A COOL ANGER BLOWING

VERNE HARRIS

MINERVA PRESS
WASHINGTON LONDON MONTREUX

A COOL ANGER BLOWING

Copyright © Verne Harris 1994

ISBN 1 85863 069 X

First Published 1994 by
MINERVA PRESS
2, Old Brompton Road,
London SW7 3DQ.

Printed in Great Britain by
Martins the Printers Ltd., Berwick upon Tweed

A COOL ANGER BLOWING

To Pat Cole-Bowen, for being cool for so long.

ABOUT THE AUTHOR

Verne Harris was born and lived in Pietermaritzburg for twenty-seven years. Now resident in Pretoria with his wife and son, he is an archivist by profession and a freelance jazz critic. His first novel *Where They Play the Blues* was short-listed for the 1991 M-Net Book Prize.

PROLOGUE

Obituary: Philip James Maddox (1930-1992)

Philip Maddox was one of the finest jazz musicians produced by South Africa. Certainly the finest produced by Maritzburg. Inspiration and awesome dedication to the tenor saxophone took him to many countries and saw him play with many international stars.

I first met Phil in 1942 when we were schoolboys completely unaware of the music which would change our lives. We discovered jazz together, and for the next ten exhilarating years played it as if nothing else mattered. In retrospect our impact on life in Maritzburg was probably marginal, but for a lot of people jazz made Maritzburg a swinging place to be in those years.

From the outset Phil was passionate about bebop. His life became a single-minded exploration of this great musical form. He would play anywhere and with anyone in pursuit of his passion. His disregard for racial and other divides was a rebuke to those of us who pandered to the social conventions of the time.

In 1955 he left Maritzburg for Los Angeles and the Bobby Ryder Band. His six-year residence there established him as a major figure on the West Coast jazz scene. He was recognised not so much for his originality as for his sustained interpretation of the bop idiom.

An invitation from Ronnie Scott took him to London in 1961. A period of consolidation followed, but in the late sixties his career lost direction. He did some experimental work, collaborating briefly with West Indian alto saxophonist Joe Harriott, but he produced nothing really worthwhile. A debilitating drug habit and the break-up of his marriage to the lovely Patty marked a further decline in his fortunes.

But in 1972 he surfaced in Paris, his life together again and rededicated to the ideals which had taken him to the top. With fellow survivors from the bop era and young French musicians of the hot neo-bop school, he blew his soul back into the vigour he had enjoyed in the 1950s. His timing was perfect, a revival of mainstream jazz soaking up his energies in a profusion of live and recorded work. This was undoubtedly the most productive period of his career.

He shifted his base back to London in 1977, from where he travelled widely throughout the 1980s. While never quite recapturing the achievements of his Paris sojourn, he maintained the highest standards of creativity.

Two years ago he visited South Africa for the first time since 1955. He came with singer Faith Woolmer, another product of the 1950s Maritzburg jazz scene. Seeing him again was a great experience. He had gone so far, achieved so much, and yet he still possessed the vitality we shared as kids. The old urgency to say something significant in his music hadn't left him. He was still a rebuke to me.

It is hard to believe that this strong life has ended. Those who were close to him will miss him sorely - Faith Woolmer; his daughter Lauren; Patty, with whom he maintained a friendship to the end; and the other members of the Now Bop Quintet, which was on tour in Europe when the last bout of pneumonia struck.

I will miss him. All who have come to respect his playing will miss him.

Gladstone Collins
Capital News
11 February 1992

PART I

SUMMER 1952-3

CHAPTER 1

For me, avoiding uncool behaviour is the most important thing. Raise a sweat, get angry, punch some idiot in the chops, but don't lose control. Stay with yourself. Being cool is *the* redeeming feature. Take Miles Davis for example. I don't dig his approach to music: it is too deliberate, cerebral. The man's horn has no passion. But it expresses the character of the coolest man in jazz; it's as pure as his hates, as immaculate as his suits. So I respect it, and sometimes, usually around two in the morning, with a half dozen brandies warm in my belly, I even begin to dig it.

These are strange thoughts to be thinking in a place where being cool seems to have no meaning. Night is stretched around me in an intensity of silence that has a sound of its own. Something you never experience in town, you know. I ease a Texan from my breast pocket and light up, but it fails to settle my thoughts. Its flavour is extracted by the gentle movement of air before I can enjoy it.

Jeeze, what a weird night this is turning out to be. Behind me, in the large farmhouse a couple of hundred yards up the drive, is a group of strangers - except for Peter - acting out an absurd protest against the government. I suppose they feel intimately engaged with a world that cannot be more real. And here I am, God knows where, disengaged in every bloody sense of the word - even from the tangible world around me.

A sudden, unreal boom frightens the hell out of me. I stop walking, and try to locate the source of the noise which has assaulted me from the dark. It takes a few moments before I realise it is a cow. I can feel sweat on my palms as I drag heavily on the Texan, then flick it in an arc towards the bovine smudge some yards from the drive.

***

It was right after work that Peter arrived at the flat. Patty wasn't back from the office yet, and I had just put a disc on the turntable. He had come to ask a favour. I knew immediately it was a big one by the way his elegant, lawyer's fingers played with the gold ring on his left hand.

"Philip, I am in a spot of bother. A lift I had arranged for tonight has fallen through, and I must get to a place out of town urgently..."

"Sure dad, can do. Where are you going?"

Peter's long body was folded awkwardly into the low chair. He looked like a man in need of a drink.

"Philip, it's a long story. Look, I cannot tell you where, nor why, in fact." He swept a wave of blonde hair back from his forehead, then stood up, his weak leg pushed forward by the movement of the strong one. "All I can tell you is that it has to do with politics, that the police would be delighted to know about it..." - he paused, his hand straying again to his head - "and that your assisting me would contribute to the cause of freedom in this country."

I tried hard to put a solemn expression on my chops. "No problem, dad. You put petrol in the Morris, and I'll ask no questions. Now, on a more serious note, what would you like to drink?"

I left a suitably vague note for Patty, and we headed for Peter's place. I parked my heap at the foot of the outside staircase which leads directly to the mansion's upper storey.

"Another imposition, old man," he said. He was more relaxed now. "For the benefit of other persons, we are taking furniture to a colleague of mine." He smiled boyishly.

I nodded, conspiratorially. "Not exactly a Raymond Chandler scene, but close enough for me."

We loaded a small table and two chairs onto the back seat, then made our way through town. The street lights were on, but were pale beneath the washed blue of the sky. By the time we had climbed through the forest north of town, the heap complaining all the way in third gear, they had achieved a respectable illumination in the valley behind us.

It was dark when we reached Howick. We stopped beside a large bungalow, orange light falling onto a lawn from two front windows. Peter got out, and limped quickly to the front door. He was admitted immediately by a chick who seemed to be worth looking at. I got out to stretch my legs, feeling more like a chauffeur than I had before we stopped. The Howick Waterfall was a distant grumble below the calling of crickets. Peter, now really relaxed, was back in a few minutes. We carried the furniture into the house - no sign of the chick - and returned with a pile of tapes and a heavy piece of equipment which I recognised to be a radio transmitter.

From there we took off on a dirt road, and I quickly lost any sense of where we were. But at least I now had a good idea of what this scene was all about. Patty, like many others, always listens to the evening news in the hope of hearing the brief interruptions by propagandists of Natal separatism. These nuts urge Natal voters to reject the government at the next general election, and, if necessary, to secede from the Union. What their plan is precisely, I don't know. I haven't taken the trouble to listen to them.

It must have been the incongruity of my position which made me curious: "You think this will achieve anything?" I asked, stabbing a thumb over my shoulder at the transmitter.

"It must," Peter replied grimly. "The Nationalists are intent on reducing English-speakers to second-class citizens and taking South Africa out of the Commonwealth."

I felt instinctive aversion. The world of politics, dominated by powerful men without hearts, is built on posture and deceit. "Jeeze dad, what the hell difference does being in the Commonwealth make anyway? And what is first-class citizenship?"

Peter took a moment to gather his thoughts. I watched the artificial foreground sculpted by the headlights rushing towards us and into oblivion. "We are fighting for freedom - political, economic and cultural."

"Balls!" I thought. What does a saphead like Peter Collins know about freedom? You find freedom inside yourself or not at all. But I said nothing. There was no way that we were going to connect.

When we arrived at the farm there was a group of cars clustered before the house. Peter turned to me: "Um, Philip old man, this is rather awkward. I think it best that you don't see any of the other people. Would you mind staying out here while we... you know...?"

"Sure dad."

"Thank you. Look, I'll bring you a drink and a bite to eat in a mo'."

I walked off down the drive.

***

I've got to know this God-forsaken farmyard pretty well by now.
I move from the drive onto the expansive front lawn. It is bordered
on all sides by flower-beds. I can smell various scents, now that my
Texans are finished. Flowers are not my scene. For whatever reason
nature has never knocked me out. I suppose there must be a wealth of
colour around me, but I can see none of it. Funny thing that.
Nothing possesses inherent colour. You see whatever light rays are
not absorbed by objects. Right now only a barely perceptible grey is
not being absorbed by the flowers.

Maybe that's why I dig the night. Things are more peaceful, not
so busy reflecting a thousand variations of light. There is less to
distract your imagination and dissipate your concentration. You can
focus more fully on... whatever: your chick, your horn, your desires.

and they could hear her humming. They reached the bathroom window. She was sitting in the bath, her arms raised to her shampooed head. Her breasts, glistening, were splendidly hung exotic fruits. Philip's gaze fixed on her nipples.

"Jeeze," he whispered involuntarily. "Jeezus."

The areolae were unimaginably dark, spread generously around the elongated breasts.

Philip felt dizzy; his breath was shallow. In that moment serendipity, until then just a fascinating word, was realised by him. But before he could recognise this, she saw them.

CHAPTER 3

The fat man stood before the opened door. He wore an expression of discomfort.

"Mr Maddox? Please excuse me. My name is Fat Singh." His hands reassured one another behind his back.

"Yeah."

Philip looked down at the fat man from behind his dark glasses. Music flooded out the doorway and into the late afternoon. Clouds were building tall in the horizontal rays of the sun.

"I am a great admirer of your playing." He coughed, a chubby hand raised to cover the lower half of his face.

"Yeah."

"That is why I am presumptuous enough to come to your home to ask a special favour." The fat man looked down at his shoes, which were half covered by the turn-ups of his trousers. His hands were doing more reassuring than ever.

Philip removed his glasses, and swept a hand through his brush-cut hair. "Come inside."

The flat was small, one of a pair above adjacent ground floor shops. Philip and Patty had been renting it since their wedding six months previously. Before then Philip had lived in a succession of boarding houses, driven on by the hostility of fellow-tenants towards his jazz records, always played at high volume, and his saxophone.

Fat Singh stood awkwardly in the centre of the lounge. He was attempting not to appear curious. The room was shabbily furnished and untidy. An ironing board heaped with washing dominated the floor. An unstable-looking easy chair, two dining room chairs and a packing case provided seating. A single yellowing print decorated the longest wall. Records, most of them in brown paper covers, were spread in disarray before a squat hi-fi unit.

"A drink?" Philip asked.

"Thank you, Mr Maddox. A glass of water please." Fat Singh was a teetotaller.

When Philip returned with the water, he was still standing, his hands behind his back.

"Take a pew, you're making me nervous."

Fat Singh grimaced, uncertain of whether Philip's invitation was meant to be humorous. He could feel sweat sliding down his temples. He turned to a chair, but seeing a dress crumpled on it, hesitated. Philip scooped the dress onto the floor and motioned him to sit down.

"So, what's your scene?"

"Mr Maddox, I am a jazz enthusiast. It is my great hobby. I do not play an instrument myself, but I promote a number of bands. Most of their work is downtown and in the locations. You have not perhaps heard of me?"

Philip shook his head. Jazz in Pietermaritzburg was delineated sharply along racial lines. White musicians seldom played with black musicians, and rarely to mixed audiences. Their world reflected faithfully the segregated nature of South African society. This pattern was breaking down in Johannesburg and Durban, but Philip's experience was restricted to Pietermaritzburg and the odd gig at clubs in Durban.

"Things are very tough," Fat Singh continued. "Work is hard to come by, and the pay is poor. Last year I organised a competition for bands at the Lotus Hall, for exposure you see? It was most successful, and now..."

He stopped speaking, and levered himself clumsily to his feet. Patty had entered the room.

"Hello," she greeted him, a hand held out. "I am Patty, Phil's wife. Don't mind me, I just want to get on with my ironing."

She smiled at him. Her small body bore a heavily swollen belly. She shuffled a few steps before turning to Philip.

"Phil, do you mind if I turn the music down a bit?"

He grunted assent.

Fat Singh pulled a large handkerchief from his breast pocket and drew it across his forehead.

"You were saying," Philip said to him.

"Yes, um, yes." He sat down. "I wish to arrange another competition, this time in Sobantu Village. My special request is that you be kind enough to be chief judge for it."

Philip raised his eyebrows, but said nothing.

"Your presence there would add prestige to the event, Mr Maddox. You have a big reputation."

"Thank you, but no thanks," Philip said. He found the idea of bands competing against one another distasteful. It violated the spirit of jazz. "I'm not the right person, you know. I'm no good at comparing musicians, and speaking in front of a crowd like that..."

"You wouldn't have to say anything, Mr Maddox. I'll do all the talking."

"It's just not my scene, you know. I could approach other guys in my band for you."

"Please, Mr Maddox. The competition is just for the audience, a way of stimulating interest. For the musicians the exciting thing would be having someone like you there, and having the opportunity to jam with you after the formalities are over."

Philip leant back and blew a cloud of smoke from rounded mouth. "I don't know."

"Perhaps you will hear one or two really good musicians, and invite them to play gigs with you in the future," Fat Singh continued. "Jazz should break down barriers, especially now when our society is creating new ones to separate us from each other. In music colour means nothing."

"Sure, I dig what you're saying," Philip said. "But that's not my problem with this thing, you know."

"C'mon Phil," Patty said softly from the ironing board.

***

It was a warm February evening. A storm in the late afternoon had drawn the heat, but left behind an oppressive humidity. Gladstone's 1936 Ford V8 was parked outside the Maddox's flat. In the front seats were Gladstone and Philip, waiting for Fat Singh.

Gladstone was talking about tensions at Park View. He rambled on, unaware of Philip's disinterest. "The sooner this election is over the better. Then we can all return to the real world, you know." He paused while he loosened the knot of his tie. "Poor Mother, she's the buffer between us all."

Philip grunted. He was wondering what lay ahead. But not too seriously. Three neat brandies had quieted his misgivings about what promised to be the uncoolest thing he had ever done. He still did not know why he had accepted Fat's invitation.

Gladstone giggled. "Jeeze, if only you could have seen yourself last night, Phil. Man, it was classic." He laughed out loud.

At the previous night's gig the band's bass player had become involved in a protracted argument with someone on the floor. Eventually the man had climbed up onto the stage, where he met a vicious punch on the jaw from the bass player. He had staggered back, a hand grabbing Philip's sling as he fell. Philip had been pulled down to his haunches, but continued playing a riff while he eased the sling from the fingers of the semi-conscious man.

"You were cool, man, *molto* cool."

Philip grunted again. "It was a bloody good punch."

Fights involving band members were not infrequent. The most common causes were male resentment from the floor at attention being paid to female partners, and frustration either with the band's unwillingness to play certain popular tunes or deliberate distortion of them if they decided to play them. Pugilistic responsibilities usually devolved on Bertie Smit, the heavy, crew-cut bass player, although his menacing appearance forestalled the need for fist-work most of the time.

A green Morris Oxford drew up alongside the Ford.

"Good evening, Mr Maddox," Fat Singh called. He was leaning across a passenger in the front seat. Three others were crammed into the back. "Please excuse my lateness. Finding all my passengers was not easy."

"Cool. Shall we blow?" Philip replied.

They followed the Morris through town out onto the Bishopstowe road. In the distance was Table Mountain, its profile just visible against the darkening sky. Without warning they entered the unlit township. Small, hidden from Pietermaritzburg's white suburbs, Sobantu was the only black residential area within the municipal boundaries. It had been demarcated by the Town Council in 1925, after a plebiscite amongst white residents had determined its position adjacent to the town's sewerage depot.

"I've never been in one of these places," said Gladstone, craning over the steering wheel. "Have you?"

"No."

"Jesus. No electricity, and no tar."

They edged forward in second gear, Gladstone guiding the Ford around water-filled pot holes and areas of thick mud.

The community hall was a crush of humanity. A small area at the front had been cleared for the bands and the judges' table. Alongside the table was a packing case, which served as the master of ceremony's rostrum. Paraffin lamps placed in window sills provided illumination.

Philip and Gladstone sat in splendid isolation for almost half an hour before Fat clambered onto his rostrum. His stance was unlikely and his balance unsure.

"Ladies and gentlemen, good evening. Welcome ...," " - he looked down to reassure himself that all was well with his perch - "welcome to the Singh Butchery All Stars Jazz Competition." He paused for polite applause. "Our honoured guests and judges tonight are the renowned saxophone player, Mr Philip Maddox, and pianist, Mr Gladstone Collins, of the Maritzburg Jazz Quintet." More polite applause. "They will choose the champion band tonight. Without more ado, let me call to the..." he hesitated, "the stage, our first band, Sobantu's own Musical Darkies!"

Sustained, enthusiastic applause filled the hall while Fat lurched backwards off the packing case.

Each band played a set of four numbers, mostly jazz standards, but shaped by the distinctive Marabi beat and patterns. It was music to which Philip could not relate. His ears, educated by the syncopated sounds of American swing, found it alien. He stopped wondering why he had come. He knew it was because he was a saphead.

"Jeeze dad, this scene is elsewhere," he whispered to Gladstone. "I wouldn't call it jazz, you know."

Later, when the formal proceedings were almost over, he turned again to Gladstone: "You know, it's not right. Two white guys judging these black bands. I don't understand their music."

"Sure, sure," Gladstone replied. "But it's interesting. Some of these cats are really good - I mean technically, you know. And they're rooted in the New Orleans tradition." Gladstone's feeling for jazz, its history and its many currents, was more catholic than Philip's.

One musician stood out for Philip. He was a trumpeter, one of four frontmen in an Edendale band, the Ten Pioneer Swingsters. Philip was impressed by the richness of his tone, and his tight and economical phrasing. The straight lines of his blowing strained against the inflected, repetitive playing of the other frontmen. And his mood, absorbed, brooding, was in contrast to the others' joyful lyricism.

Philip sought him out as soon as the winners had been announced.
"I dug your blowing," he said.

The trumpeter nodded acknowledgement, then put out his hand: "Ray Gamede."

The audience, restrained during the competition, relaxed when the jamming started. Although the only drink in the hall was in the water bottle on the judges' table, the atmosphere was warm. Chairs were piled up against the walls, and dancers annexed the floor. Philip and Gladstone found themselves pressed into almost every number. Despite the strange musical framework they were in, and for Gladstone, the inferior, tinny instrument in front of him, both began to enjoy themselves - finding their feet, drawing lines within new parameters, was challenging musically. The highlight for Philip was when he engineered a rendition of 'Summer Time' with only Ray Gamede and a three-piece rhythm section. There was an instinctive understanding between the two hornmen. They stated the melody together, individually laid down the improvisational challenge, briefly explored the melody's boundaries together, then, finally, brought the number to rest. Both men were exhilarated. Neither gave a damn that their blowing had cleared the floor of dancers.

After the session was over, a small group of musicians chatted in a huddle outside the hall. Above them was a clear sky, beneath them a thin layer of mud churned by numerous feet. Fat Singh hovered around them, delighted at the success of the evening, but eager to get going.

"Why don't we all go to Twiggy's Pie Cart for some chow?" Philip asked. He felt good. Unreservedly alive.

A collective hesitation followed his question. Then Ray Gamede spoke:

"Thank you Mr Maddox. But it is late, and we have a long way to go." He glanced around at the others. "And it is maybe a bad idea. The police can get very angry with natives in town late at night."

"C'mon dad, we'll be around." Philip gestured at Gladstone.

Ray Gamede shut his eyes, as if to deflect the attention focused on him, and shook his head. Philip was about to respond, but the trumpeter forestalled him.

"No." It was a statement of rebuke. "Once I was caught in town late. For no reason they arrested me; kept me at the station all night." He snorted. "What is the use of carrying your pass with you?" Then, raising his instrument case to Philip in a final reinforcement of the rebuke, "They damaged my trumpet man, just for a joke."

***

Philip and Gladstone were silent as they made their way back into town. Their thoughts were gnawing on Ray Gamede's story. The contour of society blazoned by it had never been considered seriously before by either of the two men. And neither possessed the means to contextualise the incident, nor to discuss it with each other comfortably.

They stopped at Park View to pick up a record which Philip wanted to borrow. In the kitchen they were both overtaken by hunger, and satisfied it by devouring a packet of biscuits. The food restored their spirits. They talked about the evening.

"Ray Gamede is something else," Philip said. "You know, 'Summer Time's' been stale for me since God knows when. But tonight, I don't know, it came alive."

"He has loads of talent. He could take it anywhere," Gladstone said.

Philip began to hum a tune. Gladstone joined him, elaborating the melody.

The kitchen door opened. It was The Judge. "It is time you young men started *behaving* like men," he said. He tugged at the lapels of his silk dressing-gown before swinging around and disappearing into the dark interior of the house.

CHAPTER 4

I suppose we all need ties to help us make sense of our lives. And not only with people. Also with places, the dead, God. Trouble is, most people find meaning in the number and range of significant ties they can make. That bothers me. Whether we like it or not, ultimately meaning has to be something we work out ourselves from within ourselves. Maybe I think like this just because I'm socially not well adjusted, you know. But the fact is, at the end of the road we are alone: the closest ties in the world don't register with death.

I have ties. I mean, jeeze, I've got Patty. And Gladstone. And the cats in the band. Close relationships. And then the deeper connections made through my sax: with my own sub-conscious; with fellow musicians in the fleeting, intense world of communal creation; and, this may sound weird, with the slave hollering his pain on some Southern plantation. Jazz, you know, *is* my life. And my sax is *the* copula in it.

When Gladstone and I started out with our trio back in '46, jazz was swing. For us anyway. We were shaped by the big bands of the '30s. We dug them all, but especially Count Basie's. The white bands, Goodman, Artie Shaw, the Dorseys, were smooth, their sound diluted by commercialism. Instinctively we knew that the Negro bands, and pre-eminently Basie, had stayed in touch with New Orleans and beyond, back to the slave plantations and the birth of the blues.

Then came bop. For me the way had been prepared by Lester Young, that greatest of all tenor saxophonists. I was dazed for days after I first heard him. His cooler, less direct approach, still energised by passion, knocked me out. It will always knock me out. The first bop recordings, it seems to me, were a logical progression from it.

From '51 we started shaping our sound into that of a bop band. Our biggest problem was getting a flexible, creative rhythm section. We finally achieved that by replacing Greasy Aubrey on drums and acquiring Bertie on bass. With the addition of Johnny's guitar last year, and Gladstone doubling up occasionally on clarinet, we had a reasonable range of horns to explore the space for the telling individual statement which the bop revolution has opened up. The other big bop innovation, the shift of improvisation from a melodic to a harmonic source, we are still working on. We're short on technique, devoid of direct exposure to the greats, and some of us don't have the dedication to really get anywhere musically. But we're moving in the right direction.

Of course, bop is not what most people who end up listening to us want to hear. Glen Miller, maybe Benny Goodman, is about the closest they've come to mainstream jazz. So compromise is essential. We play a lot of popular stuff, do as many requests as we can stomach, keep the solos within strict limits. Also, for most gigs we draft in a vocalist - at first I kicked against this, but the chick Gladstone came up with has good pipes and, thank God, she swings. So, we make enough dough to remain a going concern, and we get by, most of the time, with a minimum of tensions between us.

Friction, I would have to concede, usually centres on me. Although Gladstone is the band leader, I tend to push the band musically. Occasionally that pisses some of the guys off. And in turn I get browned off when heavy drinking and womanising affect our playing. I mean I don't give a shit what the guys do with their lives, but when they start bombing out at gigs and skipping practices, that's going too far. Fortunately, only Johnny is into drugs. And he's unusual. Even when he's as high as a coot, he stays with the rest of us. Sometimes it pushes him way ahead of us, which is cool. That's his scene, and it's part of his dedication to his horn.

Yesterday things got ugly for the first time. We were practising at our drummer's place. During a break I raised a question Gladstone and I had been discussing for the last week or so.

"Any of you cats heard of a trumpeter called Ray Gamede?"

None of them had. Gladstone and I have only played with him once before, but he knocked us out tremendously. He's one of those cats you recognise as special immediately. I told the others about him.

"What about giving him a regular blow with us?" I concluded.

The band is a bit thin up front. We recognised long ago that we need another horn, preferably trumpet or another sax.

After a long silence, our drummer spoke: "Jesus Phil, that's asking for trouble. Man, it's a jungle out there. A black frontman! People would take offence, managers would start turning us down."

Those were Gladstone's reservations. Valid too. Of course I recognise that. But what integrity would be left us by bowing to them? I expressed my feeling.

"Bullshit," Bertie responded. "We compromise left, right and centre. So don't hold up integrity as some kind of fucking icon."

I turned to Johnny. "What do you say?"

He shrugged. "I scheme maybe a Maritzburg Jazz Sextet would sound too erotic for this dorp."

I had to laugh with the others.

"Stop skirting the issue, fellows." It was Faith, our singer, who spoke. "You're just nervous this cat will steal your chicks."

"Can we be serious for a moment?" I asked.

"Sure, dad," Bertie said. "There'll be other problems as well. I mean, you know that niggers are as unreliable as hell."

I could have bust his head with my horn.

"Like I know that fat bass players are all sapheads," I said.

He advanced towards me. "Wise guy," he said. "You want to say that again?"

I took off my shades, and said it again. I was angry enough not to worry about longevity. I expected him to take a shot at my head, but he hit me in the stomach. As I folded up I twisted away from a rabbit punch and pulled him down with me. The others saved me from further damage.

"Drop the idea, Phil," Faith said to me afterwards as I drove her home.

I grunted.

"You have to be realistic. The way things are going in this country, it'll soon be illegal to have a mixed band anyway." Her hands were pushed in together between her knees. She leant forward, her head almost touching the windscreen.

I glanced at her. She is a stunning chick. Tall and dark, she looks almost Latin and possesses a quality of contained energy. Like a long, gleaming sports car. Enough to distract even the heaviest of thoughts.

"Drop it," she repeated.

Everything about her is decisive. She talks quickly. The movements of her body are quick and direct.

I thumbed my shades. "I have."

***

Apart from Gladstone - he runs *away* from chicks - the other cats have all made a play for Faith. Understandably. But she's shown no interest. She's more into the wealthy, professional kind of guy - doctors, lawyers, you know. I get the feeling she regards us as a bunch of bums. Which I suppose we are, in a sense. Not that I'm interested. She makes me nervous.

Patty is different from her in every way - small, blonde, soft-hearted, pretty quiet. And there's a measured pace to everything she does. Even when she scratches herself - slowly, almost like a caress. I dig that. A guy can really relax with her.

Weird thing, but that was the thought I had about the first woman I ever saw naked. Cousin Em. Gladstone's Cousin Em. Jesus, I remember her as if it happened yesterday. Gladstone and I were still kids, you know. Cousin Em was staying at the mansion, and we hatched this plan to spy on her while she was bathing. We climbed up piping on the outside wall, and dug her through the bathroom window. She saw us almost immediately. Gladstone ducked, but I just stood there, unable to take my eyes off her. Those gorgeous tits! Swung low, long rather than round. Nothing like I had imagined tits to be. She knew I was still standing there, but she calmly got out of the bath, dried herself, and pulled on a bathrobe. So fucking calm, as though I didn't exist, you know. My dirty little eyes just didn't *touch* her soft, self-possessed body. I still dream about it.

What that image promised, the realisation of a peace encompassing every part of me, I experienced in my first real sexual encounter. That happened not too long after the revelation of Cousin Em. I suppose I should be ashamed of it, but I'm not. Gladstone and I had spent an afternoon together preparing for school examinations at the Boys' Home where I lived. It was hot, the moisture tangible in the air. We decided to duck supper, and took off to Alexandra Park. Down by the river it was cooler. It was almost dark when we stripped off our clothes and jumped into the water. We larked about, maniacally, for a while. Then, somehow, wrestling turned into embracing. I remember hesitating momentarily, before scrambling out onto the bank. But Gladstone followed me, and on the cool grass we pursued the strange passion which had come upon us.

It never returned, and we have never discussed what happened that night. Not that I have avoided the subject - it just slipped irretrievably into the past for us, where it remains imbued, for me anyway, with an indescribable peace.

CHAPTER 5

The day was as good as done. The heat of the afternoon had passed with the sun, but it was not yet dusk. Chapel Street was still being threaded by cars and pedestrians making their way home. Some of the motorists had switched their headlamps on, but like the street lights they were unnecessary. Time seemed to pause beneath the colourless sky.

Fat Singh walked slowly towards the Maddox's flat. He was wearing a jacket and tie, his stomach pressing against the single fastened button. The end of the tie poked out beneath the button, as if unconnected to the portion knotted about Fat's substantial neck. He stopped outside a barber's shop, and gazed up at a lamp post. Like all the others in Chapel Street, it was done up with election posters. This one sported three with the same visage, and the same dreary injunction: VOTE RICHTER VOTE NATIONAL. Fat sighed, pulled a large handkerchief out of his breast pocket, and patted the sweat off his face. Mr Richter had lost to his United Party opponent the previous week, but his party had won the election with an increased majority. The narrow victory of 1948 had not been an aberration; it marked the beginning of an era. The weight of this realisation burdened Fat. He knew that the implementation of the Nationalists' *apartheid* ideology would make Smuts' harassment of Indians seem trivial in comparison.

He turned abruptly and headed for the stairwell behind the barber's shop. As he levered himself up the unlit stairs with the help of the handrail, he heard strains of exultant jazz from the flat above him. He knocked several times before the door was opened by Philip.

"Hi dad. You look as though you've had a long day." Philip leaned against the door frame, a hand straying through his hair.

Fat smiled broadly. He pointed past Philip - "Coleman Hawkins!" He had recognised the fat tone of the tenor saxophone filling the space behind Philip.

"Uhuh. The old cat himself," Philip said. "Listen, come inside."

"No thank you, Mr Maddox, I ..."

"Phil, please."

"Thank you. But I must get home. I thought I would just stop to thank you again for the wonderful job you did at the competition." His hands had found each other behind his back. "I really appreciate it."

"No sweat. It turned out to be a pleasure, you know." A hint of a smile played about Philip's mouth.

The two men looked at each other. Neither was relaxed. Fat had come on impulse, in pursuit of a vague notion that he must not allow Philip to pass him like a ship in the night. He wanted Philip's friendship.

"Tell me Fat, how can I get in touch with Ray Gamede? The trumpeter."

Fat nodded his head vigorously, a smile bunching his cheeks up towards his eyes. "You wish to play with him?"

"Sure," Philip replied.

"Ray is a very good musician. I thought you would notice him. He takes his music seriously. You will not be surprised to know that he *reads* music."

"So, where can I find him?"

"No problem. He works round the corner at Eddie's Garage in Pietermaritz Street."

***

Fat Singh was a successful businessman. In addition to managing one of the family butcheries, he had a share in the only respectable hotel in the lower end of town. It was only a matter of time before he secured sole ownership of it. Success was the fruit of dedication and acumen; he was devoid of the ruthlessness which is usually indispensable to the pursuit of profit.

Shortly before the outbreak of the Second World War, Fat's father had bought a large house in the white section of town. New Scotland Road fed off College Road and the expansive fields of Maritzburg College, led past those of Girls' High School, before winding to an end on the edge of the Msunduze Valley close to the mixed race area of Pentrich. Further along the valley was the beginning of the Edendale sprawl. The Singhs' house was one of about twenty belonging to Indians and Africans on the valley end of New Scotland

Road. They were part of the black 'penetration' into white areas so feared by most whites in Natal.

In the wake of the Population Registration Act of 1950, the whole Singh family had been classified as Asian. To their relief, for Fat had inherited his mother's tightly curled, brown hair, while Fat's youngest daughter possessed both the hair and the light skin colouring of Fat's mother. At least the classifiers had not divided the family. Fat's mother, who had died in the year before the Nationalists came to power, would certainly have been classified as 'coloured', the classifiers using the race of a person's natural father as the primary determining factor.

Fat was effectively head of the Singh home. Although retaining ownership of the butcheries, Fat's father, sickly and unable to accept the loss of his wife, had relinquished the reigns of headship. He was lonely, despite sharing the house with two sons, two daughters-in-law, and five grandchildren. As the oldest son, Fat had taken up the reigns. Now in his mid-forties, he was invested with stature by his many responsibilities - family, business, and church. He was a man of complex ties.

But it was the closeness of the Singh home which properly defined him. Home was the locus of his identity. His father had been rejected by his own family when he had eloped with a 'coloured' woman and adopted her Christianity. The Singhs had fostered a protective insularity, something reinforced by their move into a white suburb. Acceptance there was denied them, as it was in their relationships with white businessmen.

Success in business, in the church, even in his home, was not enough for Fat. He craved a broader sense of belonging. Friendship with Philip promised a step - frail, undefined, but tangible - towards realising it. This promise, given urgency by the threat of harsher Nationalist rule, underlay the vague notion which had taken Fat back to Philip.

***

Fat had not discovered jazz; it had discovered him. His father was a great fan of the American swing bands, particularly the popular white big bands which had achieved commercial success in the 1930s and 1940s. Daddy, as he was known to everyone in the extended family, had made the music part of life in the Singh home through his large collection of 78 r.p.m. records. So Fat had an ear sympathetic to jazz before ever thinking about it.

Daddy's old age was lived largely in his bedroom, and it was his records, rather than his offspring, which gave him succour. His only regular outing was to Sunday evensong in the small Anglican church in Indian town. After evensong Fat would go to Daddy's bedroom, and the two would listen to old favourites together. This was a ritual Fat had devised to make sure that he found time to be with Daddy, whom he felt he tended to neglect in the human clutter of his life.

Fat's active interest in jazz had developed late, triggered by his first exposure to jazz musicians. This occurred shortly after he bought into the Bombay Corner Hotel. At his suggestion the hotel had put on a debutantes' ball, and it had fallen to him to secure a band. Recommended by Daddy, the band had been a revelation to him. Not so much for their sound as for the milieu which they embodied. He was intrigued by their language, the spontaneity of their creativity, their beautiful instruments.

Soon Fat was organising regular dances at the hotel, at which several local bands played. The dances were good for business, but they also provided Fat with the access to the jazz scene which he sought. He talked to the musicians, made friends with a few, started listening to the music they were talking about - Count Basie, Duke Ellington, Coleman Hawkins. For a short time he managed a band, the East Street Swingers, but gigs were hard to come by, and he found organising musicians too stressful. Informal promotion suited him better.

CHAPTER 6

It was summer's reluctant farewell. A hot day late in April. Philip and Patty lay side by side on the worn carpet which covered the lounge floor, listening to the relaxed explorations of a jazz trio on the turntable. The volume was right down, for Patty's benefit. After a tiring day at the office, particularly now in the eighth month of her pregnancy, loud music was unbearable. They could still feel the heat absorbed by the corrugated iron roof pressing down into the room. Patty was wearing only panties and a shirt of Philip's. It barely stretched over her stomach.

Philip rolled over onto his side, supporting himself on an elbow. He lit up a cigarette, and watched her through the smoke which he allowed to slide out his nostrils. The exquisite burning sensation fed his sense of physical well-being. He placed the cigarette carefully in the ashtray at his elbow, and held his hand over her closed eyes. Then allowed his fingers to drop, gently, onto the lids. She moaned approval.

"This is a mystery to me," Philip said. "How can someone as big as a whale still be so beautiful?"

She caught one of his fingers between her teeth. "Thank you, arsehole."

"Seriously honey, you look great."

She drew his finger into her mouth, murmuring her pleasure.

"Fat Singh popped in again yesterday afternoon. I forgot to tell you," Philip said.

She pulled his finger from her mouth, slowly, pressing its tip momentarily between her full lips. "Do you still think he's a smooth operator?"

Philip's hand strayed down to the cigarette, now almost burnt out behind a crooked length of ash. He took a short drag before killing it. "No. He's very square, you know, but he really digs jazz, no question. And he has a good heart." Philip pulled out another cigarette.

"Mmm, I think he's humble... first impression anyway." She pulled a cushion towards her and placed it under her head. "So why did he come?"

"To thank me again," Philip said, shaking his head.

"Can I have just one puff, Phil?" She had stopped smoking when she fell pregnant.

"No."

"Hard man!" Her pale blue eyes danced. "Give me a kiss then."

He kissed her.

"Now I want to ask you something which might make you cross," she said.

He blew three perfect smoke rings over her stomach.

"Well?" she asked.

He shook his head again, a mock stern expression on his face.

"Arsehole," she said. Then laughed, a small, happy laugh. "Why don't you leave the band? They don't appreciate you. Except maybe Gladstone."

The music had stopped. Philip got up, and flipped the record over. He turned back to Patty, hands in pockets. After a long pause, he said, "And then?"

"Approach this trumpeter you like so much. Set up something with him. Maybe Fat Singh could help you."

"I can't drop the cats in the can, honey."

"Come on Phil, they don't give a shit about you. And that animal Bertie - I never want to see him again."

Philip raised a hand to his face, grasped his clean-shaven chin, then returned it to his pocket. "Bertie can't help himself, you know. Anyway, I provoked him into it."

Patty lifted an arm towards him. "Come back here, Phil."

He took her hand and sat down. He sighed. "I've been thinking about it, you know, pros and cons... jeeze." He sighed again. "There's no money outside the white scene. And with you stopping work now, we're going to need every cent we can get. In itself, that's enough to keep me in the band. But there are other things too. I mean, we're the only bop set-up in this dump, and we're good, good enough to keep me growing musically, you know. That's bloody important to me." He was prodding a forefinger into the carpet, following the edges of a wine stain. "And anyway, I don't even know Ray Gamede. I dig his horn, and he seems to be a cool cat, but that's not enough to break up something I've been building for a fucking long time."

Patty lifted her shirt, and placed his hand on her stomach. She began to trace patterns along his fingers. The music stopped.

After a long silence, Philip said, "I'm going to try and get to know him."

He moved his hand from her stomach to her chest. Then gently cupped one of her swollen breasts.

"I love you," she murmured.

He bent down and kissed her forehead.

"Stimulate me, Phil."

His hand moved slowly up the mound of her stomach, paused at her navel, descended the steepness to her pubes.

***

Phil had met Patty late in 1951. The band, then still a trio, had been in Durban for a weekend to do two gigs at the Assembly Hotel. All three of them, even Gladstone, had women with them. On the Saturday they piled into Gladstone's Ford - Philip and his date in the dicky seat - and headed south at Gladstone's habitual high speed. The decision to picnic on a beach had been a collective one, Philip being a reluctant participant. All out doors intimidated him, but beaches particularly so. Armed with dark glasses, a book, and a bottle of brandy, he faced the sand and the sun with stoic endurance.

They stopped at a deserted beach close to Amanzimtoti. While the others stripped off to bathe, Philip propped himself against the picnic basket, opened his book, and attempted literary transmigration.

"C'mon Philip, at least take off your shoes," his date said.

Philip shook his head.

"What's wrong Phil, you afraid of crabs?" Greasy Aubrey laughed.

"Ah, piss off," he mumbled.

They did.

After several pulls at his bottle and a few pages of Raymond Chandler, Philip began to feel better. He hardly noticed the shouts and giggles coming from the water thirty yards away. The endeavours of private investigator Philip Marlowe, another creature of the night, were absorbing.

Pausing to ponder a surprising twist in the plot Philip looked up, and saw two of the women fling their bathing suits on the sand before running back into the water. He grunted. One of them was Greasy Aubrey's date, a quiet blonde called Patty Brennan, whom he had barely noticed till then.

He attempted to get back into the novel, but was too distracted. He watched the five figures frolicking in the shallows until they began to make their way back. One of the naked women snatched up her towel and wrapped herself in it. The other, the blonde, casually dried herself while the others walked ahead. Philip could not take his eyes off her. Her ease, her breasts surprisingly large for her small frame, called up powerfully the image of Cousin Em. He wished he could erase the others and everything in that absurdly harsh environment except the deep ocean; meet her without words, and find peace in the body which seemed to know no shame.

He felt sick. Perhaps the sun and the brandy had something to do with it, but a week later he was still feeling sick. Obsessed, he had found out from Gladstone where he could find Patty, and one lunch time had gone to the legal firm where she worked as a secretary. He had asked for her at reception. She came through to the waiting-room, to find him standing awkwardly, trying to appear interested in an English landscape on the wall.

"Why, Philip! Hello."

He turned to her, taking off his dark glasses. "Patty. Listen, can I talk to you?"

She nodded. "Where?"

He glanced at the receptionist. "I don't know." He sighed. "Patty, how serious are you about Aubrey?"

She laughed. A soft laugh, but not nervous. "Philip, why don't we go and have some coffee or something?"

On the way to the coffee shop tucked away from Church Street in Theatre Lane, her small hand had found his. There had been no need to say anything.

***

It was after midnight. Patty had gone to bed, leaving Philip slouched in their easy chair with a brandy and Budd Schulberg's *The Harder They Fall*. The ashtray perched on the narrow arm was overflowing, its contents neatly divided into hemispheres of butts and ash. Philip closed the book, and swallowed the last of his third brandy. He was entranced by Schulberg's powerful depiction of the corrupt world of American boxing, but knew that he needed a reasonable sleep. Otherwise the workshop, where he had ground out a living as an electrician for the last four years, would be more of a trial than it normally was. Philip dreamed of becoming a fully professional musician, as much to escape the tedium of his work as to do more often what he most enjoyed doing.

"Ah, what the hell," he said to himself, retrieving the bottle from the floor. One more chapter.

He was still looking for his place when loud knocking shook the front door.

"Jesus." Flinging the book down he got up. It had to be one of two people: a drunken Gladstone come to share a new record with him, or a drunken Bertie wanting to make friends.

The knocking had become hammering by the time he reached the door. He opened it to find two strangers. They were plainclothes policemen.

The shorter of the two, a neat little man with severe moustaches, spoke. "Mr Philip Maddox? I am Captain Small. This," he gestured at the fleshy-faced man beside him, "is Lieutenant Brits. Security Branch. We have a warrant to search your flat."

"What for?" Philip asked.

"That would be telling," the little man said.

Philip stepped back, his glass held against his chest. He did not think to ask for a search warrant.

Patty emerged from the bedroom as the three men walked down the passage. She held her dressing gown tightly around her.

"Ah, Mrs Maddox, I trust?" the little man said.

"Phil, what's going on?"

"Nothing honey. Just a routine search." Philip said the first words that came into his head.

"Yes, routine for us, you understand." The little man smiled at her.

Lieutenant Brits disappeared into the bedroom as the others entered the lounge. Patty sat down in the easy chair, her legs folded underneath her. Philip stood behind her, his glass still in one hand, the other stroking her head.

Captain Small looked around the room. "Drinker, smoker, reader, musician, electrician. A man of diverse interests." The smile had not left his face. "Tell me, Mr Maddox, are you interested in politics as well?"

"No."

"Good. Very good."

He knelt down in front of the bookcase. He removed the books one by one, and placed them in neat piles on the floor. "You enjoy detective novels, don't you?"

Philip sipped at his brandy, and levelled a blank stare at the little man's forehead.

"And philosophy. And poetry. Mmm, an intellectual electrician."

Patty felt Philip's hand clench. She reached up and began to stroke it.

The little man watched them. "How well do you know Peter Collins?" he asked.

"Quite well," Philip replied.

"Are you friends?"

"I play in the same band as his brother."

"Yes, indeed. But you've known all the Collins brothers since you were a boy, not so?"

"Yes."

"But you are not his friend?"

"No."

"Ah, I see. You are very particular in your use of words."

The little man completed his search through the books, and turned to Philip's hi-fi equipment. "You would not deny that you know a lot about radios?"

"So?"

"I ask the questions, Mr Maddox."

He went through the record collection in the same way as he had dealt with the books. Then stood up, broadened his smile for an instant, and wandered around the room. He stopped in front of them. "May I have a look at what you are sitting on, Mrs Maddox?"

She stood up, and he pressed the padding, pushed his little fingers down the back and sides of the seat, then knelt down quickly and had a look under the chair.

He was on his haunches when Lieutenant Brits appeared in the doorway. Brits shook his head in response to the little man's enquiring glance.

He stood up. Straightening his tie, he said, "One final question, Mr Maddox. Where do you keep your tape recorder and tapes?"

"As you can see, I only play discs."

"Indeed, indeed. Well, thank you both for your co-operation. That will be all."

Philip and Patty sat in silence for a long time after the two men had left. He was perched on the arm of the chair, one hand still clutching his glass, the other on Patty's shoulder.

"Why, Phil, why?" She began to weep.

"I don't know, honey, I just don't know." He wondered how much they knew about Peter's political activities.

"It must have something to do with Peter Collins," she said.

"I don't know."

Patty covered her face with her hand. "Those bastards have spoilt the flat, Phil. It will never be the same again."

***

The police did not return to the Chapel Street flat, nor did their enquiries positively link Peter Collins to the clandestine radio broadcasts. Patty made the connection between the search and Philip's evening out with Collins, but Philip stubbornly refused to be drawn on the subject. The most he would concede was that the lift he had given Collins probably explained the police's interest. Reluctantly Patty let the matter rest.

CHAPTER 7

I have given up hope of getting any kip tonight. After the cops left, we sat in the lounge for about an hour, Patty mulling over every word that little shit said, me sticking to vague comments. I made us some coffee and put on Patty's favourite disc, an album of songs by June Christie - the *Misty Miss Christie*. That warm voice and the familiar tunes re-affirmed our claim to the flat. Eventually weariness overtook Patty, and we came to bed. She fell asleep immediately, her head, so small, so vulnerable, against my chest.

It's not worry keeping me awake. Well, not serious worry anyway. The little captain is sharp, you know, but he obviously hasn't got a thing on me. It's a memory. One of those mean, irritating memories that fester just beyond the grasp of one's consciousness. And in reaching back for it I have dislodged a host of others, the clarity of which is distracting me, heading me away from that unlabelled and misplaced file in my mental archives.

***

During the War Pietermaritzburg was quite a big military centre. The dump was full of soldiers from all over the place - British, Australians, New Zealanders, Poles, Canadians, South Africans. Not my scene - boy scouts was barely tolerable; the real thing a prospect of hell. But for most schoolboys it brought a world of heroism and adventure right to their doorsteps. And, I must admit, it pumped a bit of energy into Sleepy Hollow.

There were three camps just outside town - the Hay Paddock Transit Camp, the Oribi Hospital Camp, and the Durban Road Prisoner of War Camp. The Transit Camp was the most popular amongst schoolboys. From the perimeter fence they watched drill and other training, heard exciting stories from those who had already been 'up North', maybe swapped messages for servicemen's sweethearts in town. But Gladstone and I never went near Hay Paddock. We hung out at the POW camp. Situated on a ridge to the east of town, it had a great view across Sleepy Hollow to the forested hills in the west and the lonely, bald head of Swartkop Mountain. Not that we went there for the scenery, but some of the prisoners we talked to appreciated it.

There were a few Germans in the camp, but most of the prisoners were Italians. Initially it was the fact that they were prisoners that attracted us, and in a way that exotic aura endured. It seemed to invest everything they did with significance - their fiercely contested football and volleyball matches; the beautiful things they made from filched materials; and, especially, the little church they built from shale. We would watch the building operation for hours at a stretch, and although, already at the age of thirteen or fourteen, we were avowed atheists, we were as impressed as hell by the Italians' dedication. No, it was deeper than that - the church was an expression of love, without any of the shitty sentiment that is usually attached to the word.

It didn't take long before we came to dig the Italians for themselves. Weird, really, when I think about it now, because they were the antithesis of cool. They made losing control a way of life. I suppose the big thing was that they treated us like adults. Especially Roberto, whose English was bloody good, and whom we got to know well. Jeeze, I really dug him. He was the only adult I ever respected as a kid.

It must have been late in '44 that our friendship with Roberto was terminated by authority. From the outset the guards were aware of our visits to the barbed wire perimeter fence, and turned a blind eye to the sometimes less than surreptitious conversations that we conducted. But we were warned against exchanging anything with the prisoners. That didn't stop us, of course. They were always keen for fresh fruit and sweets, while we prized the finely crafted ornaments and gadgets they made. Most of these objects were made from aluminium. Roberto told us that in the first months of their incarceration a load of aluminium water bottles had been stored in the camp for shipment elsewhere. Overnight most of them had disappeared into prisoners' hiding places.

It was a weekday afternoon. As usual we had cycled from town - me on Peter's battered old Raleigh - stashed the irons when we ran out of road, and walked across the veld to the camp. We must have been careless that day, because a guard caught us pushing fruit through the fence to Roberto. After a long delay - we sat in an office, dejected at the thought that we had got Roberto into trouble - we were bundled into a jeep with our irons and driven to the police station in town. There we were given a dressing down by a cop who forbade us from going anywhere near the camp again. And that's where my memory draws the irritating blank - I just cannot detain the image of that cop, nor the content of the dressing down. But Captain Small's visit tonight won't let me release the blank. His sarcastic, self-satisfied manner keeps naming the lost file, promising retrieval but providing nothing. Was that cop Captain Small? What the fuck; why should it matter?

***

Roberto was a small man - I was taller than him - with bright black hair and ill-shaven beard that impressed the shit out of us. It was the kind of beard we hoped our fluff would become one day. Neither of us possessed razors then, you know, but were trying to hasten the day when we would need them by regularly rubbing vaseline into our faces. Jeeze, the stuff you believe when you're a kid.

One of the things we dug about Roberto was his patience in teaching us Italian phrases. We really pestered him. What is "fart" in Italian? What is the equivalent of "piss off"? That kind of stuff. But it was more than just acquiring foreign crudities. We dug the *sound* of the language. The contrast between spoken Italian and spoken English is something like the difference between Jimmy Rushing and Bing Crosby - the one's all about swing, emotion and imagination, the other is smooth, sentimental and calculating. That's my feeling about it, you know. Anyway, while we were seeing Roberto we adopted a store of Italian phrases as part of a kind of private language of our own. We lost a lot of it when we got into jazz, and I've forgotten most of it now.

Roberto was a small cat jerked out of his world by massive forces. That's the impression of him that remains with me. He hated fascism and war with the same passion. Implicit in everything he said was the belief that truth is secured through immediate relationships in a constant fight against systems - political, social, religious, whatever. He didn't give a shit about the War; surviving until he could go home was all he worried about.

He talked about home often. Before the War he had worked in his family's fish shop in Peschiera del Garda, a small village on the southern shore of Lake Garda. Jeeze, his descriptions of the place were so vivid it's almost as though I've been there. A compact, fortified island in the conjunction of river and lake. To the south the flat plains of northern Italy, to the north the long, fish-laden lake couched in the foothills of the Alps. That was *his* place, you know. Talking about it brought tears to his eyes.

He found it strange that neither of us had any sense of belonging to a place. I remember how he swung his arms about, encompassing the valley, the hills, the veld around us, and said: "But this all has given you birth!" Well, he didn't often talk shit, but he did then. I don't even know where I was born; haven't a clue who my parents are. It's different for Gladstone. He has roots as long as an elephant's trunk. But for him they dangle just like a trunk - somehow they never got rooted. Both of us feel nothing for this dump. When the big break comes, we'll be gone.

***

Patty groans in her sleep, her small fist pushing into my shoulder. I place my hand on her head, then stroke it. She groans again, softly.

Like Roberto, she has strong ties to family and place. She's devoted to her crazy family, who all live here, worse luck, and she digs this dump the most. I don't know. Maybe I'm missing some vital organ, because I have no feeling for this kind of tie.

But Patty says she'll be happy to come with me when the time comes to go. Who knows, maybe we can look up Roberto in Peschiera del Garda one day. I think Patty would dig him too.

PART II

WINTER 1953

CHAPTER 8

The notes were rough at the edges, the tone of the tenor saxophone angry. Philip was tracking over his first solo on 'Lester Leaps In', extending the improvisation, affirming his mood, like a painter filling out the lines of a sketch. He stood motionless beneath the glare of a spotlight, his expression hidden behind the lenses of his dark glasses. The Quintet's rhythm section provided a swinging, but not intrusive platform for the statements of his horn. Beside him, perched on a bar-stool, his guitar silent, Johnny van Rensburg marked the beat with sharp movements of his head. He was absorbing Philip's anger, impressed by the controlled beauty of it. When the number ended, tied together neatly by the rest of the band, Johnny opened his blood-shot eyes and briefly joined the applause from the floor.

"You're blowing just great," he said.

Philip nodded acknowledgement as he turned for his glass of brandy. He drained it, then signalled to a waiter for another one, as Johnny laid down the melody of the next number, a down tempo ballad.

They were doing their regular gig at The Blue Moon night club, a cramped building wedged between shops in Forresters Lane. Owned by a garrulous Geordie who paid generously for good music, it was a favourite haunt of Pietermaritzburg's jazz musicians and other night people. Definitely not a place for the overly comfortable and the comfortably prejudiced - always a tramp or two outside, the music too loud, the menu plain, and frequented by a growing number of 'coloureds' and Indians. It was here that Fat Singh had first heard Philip playing; here that he brought his wife and business acquaintances on special occasions. Apart from Twiggy's Pie Cart in the Market Square, it was the only place in town where a meal could be bought after ten in the evening.

The ballad ended, Philip exchanged signals with Gladstone, and the band cut loose in an uncharacteristically wild rendition of a Charlie Parker number. The rest of the band were instinctively responding to Philip's mood. And shaping it, channelling it, for their mutual understanding, which forged a unity out of the individual statements, was drawing him out of himself. Giving him the resource to lay his anger to rest.

It had been with him since lunch time, when he had ducked out of the workshop to look up Ray Gamede at Eddie's Garage. The garage had two sections, a service station and a used car sales yard. Philip had noticed Ray almost immediately - a tall, round-shouldered figure washing a car in the yard. They had greeted one another reticently, both unsure of themselves. A couple of months had passed since the competition in Sobantu.

"We're doing a gig at The Blue Moon tonight, you know. Why don't you come round for a blow?"

Ray nodded, then turned back to the green Morgan sports car, drawing a chamois leather cloth across its bonnet in short, decisive arcs.

"You know The Blue Moon?"

He nodded again. "I have heard."

"So, what do you say? We could blow up a storm together."

Ray straightened up. "Man, I have a problem." He pushed a finger into his widow's peak, and held it there. "I call you Phil?"

"Sure, dad."

"Unfortunately, how can I say, my trumpet is tied up. Pawned."

"Jesus!" Philip exclaimed.

"Like you say. My family has a bit of trouble, there is a need, so I pawned it for a time." The finger was pushing into the peak, backwards and forwards.

The two men had looked into each other's eyes. Spontaneously Philip had placed a hand on Ray's shoulder. His friends would have been surprised to have observed this, for he seldom expressed his feelings through physical contact.

Just then a powerfully built man had appeared from behind the Morgan. His eyes narrowed as he spoke. "Good afternoon, Sir. Can I help you?"

Philip's hand dropped, again without thinking. "No thanks, dad. Ray is a friend of mine."

"I see," the man replied. "Well do me a favour, bud, come back at five, okay? I don't like people interfering with my coons at work." He glared at Ray, who raised the cloth to Philip in an awkward farewell before turning back to the car. "And another thing," he said to Philip, "I'm not your father."

Confrontation would have made things worse for Ray, so Philip chose humiliation by walking away. Anger had ebbed and flowed in him all afternoon, at times concentrating into an almost physical pain. A chain of neat brandies had steadied him through the early part of the evening - not too many, and not too fast, for he refused to compromise his playing - until his horn could administer its balm.

***

The Blue Moon closed at one. Gladstone, having parked his Ford outside the flat before the gig, walked home with Philip. They strolled down the middle of Pietermaritz Street, both enjoying the night's silence and strangely intimate space. Philip was relaxed, even happy. It had been a very good blow.

"You were pretty steamed up tonight, Phil. Christ, you even turned 'Laura' into a shout."

Philip nodded.

"Want to talk about it?"

"Nah; just a bad day at the workshop, you know."

There had been a distance between them since the band's disagreement over Ray Gamede. Gladstone was aware of it, but was reluctant to broach the subject with Philip. He felt that he had let him down, and, though he would not acknowledge it, knew he had let himself down.

Philip glanced at Gladstone, mischievously. "My boss, you know, the slob. His Natal Fever is getting worse and worse. You know, if he sat down on his nuts, I think he would endure the pain rather than get up."

They both laughed. Gladstone aimed a weak punch at Philip's shoulder.

"Listen, dad, why don't you come up for a nightcap?" Philip said. "I want to play you a cut from the disc I bought last week."

"*Grazie.*" Gladstone was tired, but too pleased by Philip's warmth to refuse.

In the flat Philip cleaned the record, wedged between his chest and the fingers of his left hand, with an anti-static preener. "Gladstone, old son, this is a marriage blessed in heaven - Horace Silver and Hank Mobley."

Gladstone looked around the room. "Phil, what about the baby?"

"No problem, dad, she sleeps like a bomb."

They were listening to a second cut when Patty appeared in the doorway. She ignored their greetings.

"Jesus, Phil, what are you doing?" There were deep shadows beneath her eyes. She seemed smaller than ever in the bulky folds of her cheap gown.

They watched her in silence. Philip felt the same helplessness he had felt at Eddie's Garage.

"Either *you* take off that disc, or I will."

***

Nine months had not been long enough to prepare Philip for the baby's impact on his life. Nothing would have prepared him. She had claimed Patty, transforming her into a devoted slave and shattering the orientation of her relationship with Philip. The wonder and excitement of the birth, which had bewildered Philip, drawn him closer to Patty than he'd ever been, had dissipated in the avalanche of the baby's demands. Patty was always tired, jazz irritated her, she seemed to talk only about the baby; and she had drawn her mother, whom Philip despised, into an intimate triangle with the baby. Although Philip was aware of Patty's attempts to involve him in the baby's routine, he felt excluded. The baby, at first a hairless fat-faced creature, now hairless but pixieish, remained a stranger to him. He felt the tie, tenuous, indefinable, but it was overshadowed by the intensity of the bond between Patty and the baby.

After Gladstone's departure, Philip had walked the pavement beneath the flat, his hands deep in the pockets of his corduroy trousers. The valley air, heavy and still, was cold, but he was warm inside his chunky polo-neck jersey. He paused at the Salvation Army Hall, an absurdly pompous building which made no connection with its surroundings. Its huge classical columns, squeezed between rows of shops, seemed mean - the expression of a passionless faith. Philip climbed the broad steps beneath the row of columns, his thoughts focusing on a happy event which had happened there almost exactly a year before. He leaned against one of the columns and looked up at the stars, chips of ice he felt he could touch if only he reached up high enough.

Marriage was an institution Philip had never considered entering. He had assumed that Patty would move in with him, fashion a home, and bear children without requiring society's formal recognition of the arrangement. He had submitted reluctantly to her insistence on an engagement ring before making love without a condom, and on a church wedding rather than a brief visit to the magistrate's office. His consolation was a swinging party for friends at the flat instead of a reception in the Brennan's home.

And the party *had* swung, through the night and to an end on the steps of the Salvation Army Hall. The survivors had abandoned the debris in the flat at about five in the morning to watch the dawn and greet the morning's first pedestrians. Philip remembered huddling under a blanket between Patty and Faith, deep in a tequila-inspired fellowship. It was well with the world - this was the best wedding he had ever been to, and marriage seemed sublime. Faith, very solemn, and very unsteady, had leaned forward and looked at each of them in turn: "Darlings, you have done an arseholeish thing, but I know you will be fine. Look after each other." And she had kissed them both; lingering, lipsticked kisses on the mouth.

***

Our pasts are either our friends or our enemies. We can deny them, embellish them, flee them. But we cannot discard them. As long as we have memory, we are tied to them in a most intimate relationship.

Like all close ties this one can so easily become a fetter. It happens as soon as we admit domination, of our past by us, of us by our past. The balance, so fine, so volatile, was realised instinctively by Philip. His past was a chord sequence upon which he improvised his present, a rhythm sustaining his explorations.

CHAPTER 9

We have a great shithouse. It has style and atmosphere. The walls, painted by some crazy bastard who must have spent a lot of time in here, are canary yellow. Taped onto the back of the door, which is the same canary yellow, are magazine photographs of Mae West, Humphrey Bogart and Charlie Parker. From behind the occupant of the throne, rising from the butcher's shop below, comes the hum of a motor. Every few minutes it rattles convulsively, as if clearing its throat. Atmosphere, you know. I dig this joint the most.

And, like the painter, I spend a lot of time in here. For me the word toilet has a special resonance - I *toil* on the throne. Patty pops in, the quicker the better; me, I have to persuade my bowels to void themselves. Time and relaxation are the keys. And I play them by reading demanding stuff. On the miniature table next to me - made and painted Public Works Department green by Max, Patty's father - are T.S. Eliot's *Essays Ancient and Modern* and a biography of Jelly Roll Morton. And resting on my knees, a real gem, Bertrand Russell's *The Problems of Philosophy*.

I first read *Problems* in my first year out of school. Gladstone and I were working together in a hardware store, a real dump, where we styled ourselves as intellectuals sweating out a living in the mundane world. Chandler, Schulberg, Salinger and James Hadley Chase didn't suit the image. We joined the library, started reading William Blake, T.S. Eliot, Kant, you know, cats like that, as much to impress each other and the librarian as to satisfy our intellectual needs. It was *Problems* which really nailed me, cutting through the muddle and pretension I had built up from my aimless literary wandering. To be honest, I hadn't understood half the stuff we had been reading - it was the promise of profundity, the elevated energy of the writing, which had stimulated me. Russell's simple analysis of the basis of knowledge provided a framework. A great cat - the intellectual equivalent of Lester Young.

Tonight the shithouse is a refuge. Out in the flat, I can hear their voices, are Patty, the baby, and Patty's mother. I retreated here when I could take no more; if she stays much longer I'll have to duck out to The Blue Moon.

Bertha hasn't got a lot going for her, but one thing she possesses in abundance is timing. Christ! After supper, for the first time in maybe a month, Patty really wanted sex. She poured us drinks, and invited me to take a bath with her. That is a standard message - "I want closeness, exploration, sustained pleasure". I haven't received that message since before the baby's birth. I was undressing her - jeeze, her tits are so inviting these days - when Bertha knocked on the front door.

Bertha was in a state - tears, high-pitched voice, you know, the whole scene. We took her into the kitchen, and Patty boiled up some milk for a cup of ovaltine.

"Your father *hit* me, Patricia," Bertha moaned.

"Why?" Patty asked, without looking up from the stove.

"Because he's a drunkard; a pathetic wasteful of a man," she replied.

Bertha has perfected the art of the malapropism. At most times it gives me a kick.

"What happened, Bertha?" I asked.

"I was showing him the birthday present I bought for Auntie Ruth. A lovely vase; such a lovely vase." She dissolved into tears.

Patty lifted the pot from the stove, and turned to Bertha. "It's alright, Mom, it's alright." She kissed her.

"He took offence at something I said, and, and," her voice quavered, "and he threw the vase on the floor."

"And then he hit you?" I asked.

She nodded. "A *fervent* slap in the face." She dissolved again.

The ovaltine seemed to calm her down, and she was smiling when Patty fetched the baby for an unscheduled drink. That's when I ducked in here with a brandy for some shithouse therapy.

***

I was still in the shithouse when Max arrived. It's the first time that he's been to our place. The walk had sobered him up a bit. The poor old bugger played a comic game in which nothing out of the ordinary had happened. A surreal moment of peace for Bertha.

When they left, Patty attempted to revive our erotic scene, but I was as cold as a night watchman's shoes. My resentment was directed at her.

CHAPTER 10

Philip was sitting on the edge of the chair, hunched over his saxophone. The elegant Buescher was immaculate. It had taken Philip six years to save up enough to purchase it and replace the old Selmer Gladstone had given him when they started out. Grasping the barrel in his left hand, he carefully held a lighted match to the cork on the horn's crook with his right hand. After a few seconds he withdrew the match, blew it out, and leaned back. He sighed as he watched the last thread of smoke rise from the blackened head.

It was quiet in the lounge. Patty was giving the baby her early evening feed in the bedroom. Philip looked at his watch - five minutes before Gladstone was due to pick him up for a gig at a hotel ten miles out of town. He sighed again. His thoughts were drifting, resisting his attempts to contain them. Patty, where are you tonight? he thought. Far away, far from me, in a world the baby has sprung you into.

He reached down to the floor, picked up the saxophone's mouthpiece, and fitted it onto the crook. He grunted. The slightly expanded cork had secured a better fit. He leaned forward and placed the horn in its case.

Who is this baby of ours? This little girl creature with physical being, but mysterious, indeterminate personality. I cannot connect with you.

Earlier he had watched Patty bathing her, the tiny body contorting in distress, the toothless mouth wide to cry its protest. He had felt frustrated by his inability to understand why the infant was so unhappy - usually she enjoyed her bath.

Philip stood up, glanced again at his watch, then walked to the lounge window. Already his thoughts - forming, disintegrating, re-forming - had moved crazily on. An image of Ray Gamede, standing beside the Morgan sports car, chamois leather cloth in his hand, formed momentarily. How reliable are you, dad? A man who pawns his horn could have difficulty meeting his commitments. Bertie Smit's statement about 'niggers' pulsed in neon-lit crudity across his mind.

"Jesus."

Philip felt dull. He was not looking forward to the gig - the thought of wrestling with his dullness, expressing on his horn only dullness or futile wrestling with dullness, did not exactly excite him. He considered another brandy, but decided against it. Alcohol, he knew, could ease the pain, but it could not - at least in his present mood - ignite his creativity.

He stared down into Chapel Street. The lull after rush hour was over, the energies of evening, such as they were, beginning to build up. A fat, almost full moon, was sliding up into the night sky. Philip did not notice it. He was watching two women cross the street. They paused at the centre line, arm in arm, waited for a diminutive Hillman Minx to pass, then strode to the pavement directly beneath Philip. As they reached it, the taller of the two threw her head back and laughed. Her teeth were bright beneath a nearby street light. She wore a wide-brimmed hat at a steep angle.

There was a carefreeness about her which beckoned Philip. But, he realised immediately, it was a projection of his own needs, a phantom as beyond his reach as the intrinsic physical nature of the woman. After work that afternoon he had been reading Bertrand Russell in his place of perennial toil, and had grappled with the notion that the senses are capable of providing only a limited, subjective experience of physical objects. Now, contemplating the image of the woman which remained with him, he recognised that it was a coalescence of many images, reflecting her range of movement from when he had first seen her to the moment she had disappeared beneath him. Her objective physical appearance was elusive - and would be elusive to any enquiry dependant on the senses.

***

Whether dull or sharp, Philip never looked forward to the band's weekly gig at the Thornville Hotel. They were booked for a formal dance routine, so wore tuxedos and bow-ties, and stuck to a programme of popular swing numbers. Requests for tunes like 'How Much is that Doggy?' and 'On Top of Old Smoky' were numerous - the band's acquiescence was relatively generous, informed by the fact that the Thornville management provided them with their most lucrative date. As Philip put it, "We really graft for our dough".

For Philip grafting and going through the motions were synonymous. In the first set he stayed with the melody as much as possible, rode the rhythm section and let the notes blow themselves. He hung back, fast in his dullness, wary of the edge where original statement begins. He had nothing to say. Until Faith Woolmer joined the band for the last two numbers of the set.

Faith was not a great jazz singer, but she was good. Her classical training had provided her with the discipline and control within which her natural feel for jazz rhythms found expression. Although she had a tendency to overdo the vibrato in the upper registers, her tone was rich and her phrasing tight. And her personality was not overbearing. Tonight her mood - gay, humorous - was infectious, even for Philip. She took the last number of the set, 'Makin' Whoopee', by the scruff of the neck, upping the tempo and creating her own lyrics. At first Philip was irritated by the intrusion on his fastness, but gradually he began to respond to the challenge. When Faith ran out of lyrics and began to scat, something which usually bored him, Philip engaged her, tentatively at first, then in a fully-fledged musical conversation. They took a relaxed intimacy to a joyous celebration, and back again, pushing the limits of both melody and harmony. Gladstone raised a sweat trying to bring the number to a close.

At the break Philip pulled up a chair next to Faith. He was unsettled by the change in mood the music had worked in him.

"You really swang, babe," he said.

She nodded, a smile about her eyes. "You likewise."

He looked at her steadily. "Like never before, you know. I dug it the most."

"To say the least," she responded, using an old band joke.

He turned to order drinks from a waiter, then watched her as she picked up a shawl and wrapped it around her shoulders. She was wearing a dark blue off-the-shoulder dress - a match with the band's tuxedos - and her earrings, also blue, hung low down her elegantly long neck. They swung forward, catching distant lights as she drew a box of Philip Morris cigarettes to her and lit up. Her olive skin glowed in the orange illumination of the match.

"You look cool tonight," Philip said.

She smiled, shaking her head, creases spreading from her eyes to her mouth. "Jesus, Phil. A compliment."

She was surprised. Philip was the only band member who had not made a pass at her. His initial grudging acceptance of her had grown into an affection tempered by diffidence and professional respect. She liked him. His self-containment, independence, the way he moved on the periphery of the band's camaraderie, were attractive.

"So, what's up?" he asked.

"Meaning?"

Philip slid a cigarette out of his breast pocket. He took the matches offered by her, lit up, and inhaled deeply.

"Something in your eyes, you know; the same something in your singing. What's up?" he repeated.

She looked at him for a few moments, then leaned forward. "I'm leaving. You know I'm always talking about it. Now I've decided to take the leap and try to get a break in London."

For a moment Philip was expressionless. His gaze tracked up her face - the full, brightly-painted lips, dark eyes, bold eyebrows, her black, short-cut hair. He nodded. "That's great."

"You wish me?"

"Sure, babe, I wish you the world."

Their drinks arrived. Philip raised his glass. "The world," he repeated.

They drank in a short, pregnant silence.

"Fuck it, Phil, I can't take this dump anymore. Working in the chemist is a drag. Being bored by stupid, *stupid* men is a drag. And the few gigs I get, where are they taking me? Nowhere."

Philip nodded. "What about Durban? Or Joburg?"

"Phil, listen to me. This whole country is a dump, a nowhere joint. I want to get right out, breathe fresh air."

Philip drained his glass. "And get recognition."

"Sure." She leaned forward again, dropping her voice. "You should do the same. You're wasting your talents here."

He shook his head, a hand playing down the beaded sides of his glass.

"You could go right to the top, Phil," she said. "I want success, right? Jesus, who doesn't? But you want more than that; nothing less than mastery is good enough for you. And that, bud," she paused to put her cigarette out, "is your ticket."

Philip raised his cigarette between thumb and forefinger; watched the descending pink line which marked the boundary between tobacco and ash.

"This place is too small for real dedication," she continued. "It's mean, you know. You're stifled here."

He looked away. Her closeness, the smell of her perfume, her knee pressed against his, were distracting. Gladstone, sitting across the table, caught his eye and jerked his head. It was time for the second set. Philip pushed his chair back before turning to meet her gaze again.

"It's not so easy with a family, you know," he said.

"Sure," she said.

***

On the road back into town after the gig Philip hunched into the leather of the Ford's rear seat. Faith sat next to Gladstone in front, watching the narrow strip of tar being devoured at ninety miles an hour by the powerful engine. Gladstone hummed to himself, gripping the steering wheel in one hand. The others were silent.

Philip watched the back of Faith's small, sleek head. A sense of danger, of being on an emotional edge, gripped him. He was caught between desire and the dullness which for weeks had been threatening to envelop him. He desired the freedom which Faith possessed - to cast off his domestic fetters; walk out of the Electricity Department workshop; pursue a course, some course, which at once made sense musically, and included Ray Gamede. And he desired Faith herself - the person who was free, and who dug his blowing; the woman whose body was so inviting.

But he knew he was tied down. He felt he would never slip the edge. Fiercely he gripped the side-window handle and wound the window down. He thrust his face into the blast of cold air. As he did so he caught a glimpse of Faith. She had turned to look at him. Her eyes were speaking a language he understood.

CHAPTER 11

You despise some scene, and the people who are into it, for years. That habit forms an emotional and, to be honest, a moral orientation. Then, suddenly, you find yourself in it. The orientation falls apart, and you try to convince yourself that you have grown, all the while worrying like shit that you're really going down the tubes.

The first time I got stoned - after two previous unsuccessful attempts - was a revelation. Patty had taken the baby over to the Brennans so that I could get in some practising. I blew for a few minutes to get into the groove, then lit up my joint - a carefully stoked Texan. You kind of slide into the dope at the same time as it slides into you. I became aware of things happening in my head; spaces opening up, undreamt of possibilities suggesting themselves. All kinds of metaphors, none of them dramatic enough, could be used. Let's just say it was a revelation.

I became aware of changes in perspective. The walls assumed crazy angles, kind of looming into the room, forming a dynamic prism about me. My horn grew beneath my hands without threatening to become uncontrollable. A whole new terrain, with infinite subtleties, was opened to my tiny, eager hands. When I blew, the notes filled the space around me, moving into, holding, dancing with, the transformed objects in the lounge. The notes themselves were objects - they had shape and texture. Talk about a copula. The horn was connecting me, with unimaginable immediacy, to a rich, volatile tapestry of phenomena. My lips, like my hands, were small, capable of a whole range of wild embouchures. The excitement, you know, was intoxicating. Like a child pushing a hand through an exotic glass mobile, I blew notes out of the horn and into the room, and then watched the resulting chain of images dance before me. Except they were more than images - they embraced all my senses, and their movement reflected inside my head.

By the time I walked down to The Blue Moon for our gig - in the early evening, the night already dark above the streets - the excitement had abated. But not the *awareness*. I was a moving sensor, alive to a whole world we're cut off from, or cut ourselves off from, when we're straight. The textures of walls, the resonances of a myriad sounds, the subtle colours of night - jeeze, I could bore you with a whole inventory. My blowing that night was intense. The sounds drew on feeling, which fed new sounds, connecting, always connecting at all levels of awareness.

It was a dizzy experience, revelatory stuff. But it was entirely my own. The audience, even the other cats in the band, were a distant backdrop. Gladstone came round the next day to find out, as I discovered after an hour's natter, if I was okay. He knew I had been stoned.

"You really wailed, dad," he said, "but you were in a different ball park."

He was concerned. Gladstone worries about things like that, you know. I was also concerned - connecting with yourself is important, but not if it destroys other forms of communication. Since then I have learnt how to use pot. You have to control it; avoid the temptation to trip right out. The goal is to take just enough to kill inhibitions and barriers, and stir the soul.

Still, I ask myself often, every day, whether this scene is cool. In a sense I suppose it's not. You're not staying with yourself, in the way most people understand it anyway. In the way I thought of it, you know. You trip out of one world into another. Maybe it's an unreal world, but who's to say? I think Bertrand Russell would have had a whole lot more to say about reality if he had experimented with pot. The crux of the thing is that the world you enter is a very cool one. And in it you are cool. I kid you not. You are harmoniously alive to everything in it.

That's why I got into this scene. Jazz is about feelings. If you don't blow from the soul you might as well pack it in and join the Salvation Army band. You know, a lot of cats debate the merits of the hot and the cool schools of jazz in the States. The one, they argue, is about feeling and spontaneity, the other rooted in cerebral pursuits and careful arrangement. It is a false comparison; a load of crap. Take a cat like Stan Getz, the embodiment of so-called cool school sax playing. His blowing is cool, sure, but it's because he *is* a cool cat. He blows from his soul. It's when cool is an attitude rather than a feeling that it produces barren blowing, like that of all those West Coast geeks who are trying to intellectualise jazz. You try to infuse jazz with ideas, and you kill it, whether your blowing is hot or cool.

For all kinds of reasons I was down, really heavy, my soul crunched up inside me. Day after day. And that was what I blew, night after night. A real killer. Pot offered me a way back. Not a way out, you know; a way *back* to the source of my creativity. Still, it makes me nervous.

It was about a month ago that I decided to try out pot. It had been a relatively good day at the workshop; well, at least I was feeling good about it when I got home, which is unusual. A little incident in the canteen at lunch time had perked me up. My boss - a guy who thinks he's really tough - and I get on each other's tits in a big way. We were sitting opposite each other, addressing our plates of giblets. He was shovelling it in.

"Nice grub today. What is it?" he asked the guy sitting next to him.

"The insides of a chicken," I said.

He looked down at his plate, then glared at me comically, his mug still full of the stuff. He turned to the guy next to him, who nodded confirmation. After another, desolate look at the plate, he got up in a hurry and made for the door, but his sensitive stomach was too quick for his heavy legs.

That evening I was feeling positive; I was with myself. I played with the baby while Patty had a bath, then I made us scrambled egg for supper. We chowed on the lounge floor, listening to a Frank Sinatra disc. I started getting randy.

"Not tonight, Phil," Patty said to me. "I'm really pooped. Lauren niggled all day again. I think I'm going to go straight to bed." She put a hand on my knee.

I pulled out a Texan, trying to find a reserve of reasonableness as I went through the lighting up routine. I failed.

"Sure. I'm used to it," I said.

We looked at each other across a distance I think we both felt opening up irreversibly. Weariness, and the prospect of weariness, dulled her eyes.

"You regret having had Lauren, don't you, Phil?"

She was right, but I didn't admit it. "That's crap," I said.

Patty withdrew her hand; let it stray through the straggled ends of her hair. I wonder what she saw in my eyes.

"*I* regret it. Perhaps we weren't ready for it." Tears spilled down her cheeks. "I love her, Phil, but she is pulling us apart."

I was nailed. The moment demanded honesty and tenderness, but they eluded me. For a long time we sat in a silence disturbed only by the needle tracking the groove's end. It seemed to measure the distance between us. Eventually Patty got up, touched my head, and was gone.

I sat motionless, listening to the needle. It might have been then that the idea of trying pot germinated. But maybe it happened later, when I was down in the streets trying to walk out my frustration. Whatever. After finding myself at the Bombay Corner - I had hoped to see Fat, but he wasn't in - I headed for Johnny van Rensburg's place. He stays in a room in the backyard of his parents' house up near the station. I didn't hang around long, although Johnny tried to persuade me to share a joint with him. For some reason I wanted to be alone when I first tried the stuff.

Back at the flat, I shut myself in the shithouse and lit up. I was pretty nervous, you know, not knowing where the hell it was going to take me. I sat staring at the picture of Charlie Parker, feeling close to the big man and wondering if he had also smoked his first joint in a shithouse. Well, nothing happened. That joint left me as straight as shit.

Needless to say, I felt pretty flat. After jerking myself off, which made me feel worse, I sloped to bed. Patty groaned in her sleep, then snuggled up against me. Christ, I felt rotten.

***

Patty's initial reaction to this scene was fear. Not disapproval, nor even disappointment. She's not that type of chick. She was afraid that I was going to destroy myself. But she put no pressure on me, you know. Maybe that's just another indication of how far apart we are these days, but I don't think so.

Now she is more at peace with it. She can see that I have it under control, and that it's doing a lot for my blowing. And, I think, I'm easier to live with. On one occasion I tried to persuade her to smoke a joint with me, but she refused.

"Not with the baby, Phil," she said. And then, after a long pause, "Anyway, I don't *need* it. You're an artist, and you need special stimulation. Right now you're not getting it, from me or anything

else. I'm just an ordinary person. I get enough stimulation from
ordinary things."

Like the baby, I wanted to say, but kept it to myself.

CHAPTER 12

The room was illumined by the slanted rays of the late afternoon sun. A parallelogram of light, shifting with the movement of the heavy floral curtains, patterned the carpet at the feet of Ray Gamede. He sat upright in the high-backed chair, eyes closed, his trumpet resting in vertical position on his knees. His body was motionless, reflecting his absorption in the chorus being played by Philip - a restrained but warm interpretation of the beautiful 'Tangerine'.

Philip was sitting alongside him, on an identical chair, but with strikingly contrasting posture. One leg crossed over the other, his saxophone held low on his right side, he was hunched forward into the horn. The instrument, catching light from the window with every movement, was an extension of his body, a channel for the energy flowing up his torso. He was relaxed but sharp, a balance, though he tried to convince himself otherwise, he seldom achieved when doped up. Today he had got it right, and the depth of his feeling was being translated into a sound which captivated Ray.

Opposite them, providing the two hornmen with the rhythm, was a bass player and a drummer. James du Bois, a Mauritian by birth, was an unusual bass player by Pietermaritzburg standards - he was short and left-handed, and possessed an accomplished technique. His powerful hands manipulated a strong, swinging stream of notes. His head, topped by a maroon beret, was bent close to the strings.

In both mood and skill, the drummer was set apart from the others. Jackie, a 'coloured' with Eastern slanted eyes and almost permanent grin, moved about frenetically on his stool. Using brushes, on the insistence of Philip, he attacked the sparse set of instruments in front of him - base and snare drums, cymbal and high-hat. Mouth wide open, he looked around the room constantly, often catching the eye of the room's other occupant, Fat Singh.

It was Fat's room - the expansive lounge of the New Scotland Road house which Daddy Singh had bought in 1939. Fat was slouched back in an armchair not designed for slouching. He looked uncomfortable, discarded, but he was happy. His friends were making music in his home, testing themselves and each other. He absorbed the energies of the jam session like a sponge, and they worked in him an intense sense of well-being. His feet, imprisoned in shining, sharp-pointed shoes, marked the beat with awkward sideways movements.

There was a long pause after the number ended. Ray turned to Philip and nodded, a wide smile engaging his whole face. Then simultaneously they bent to retrieve glasses of beer.

Fat levered himself up in his chair. "Super playing. I would say exceptional," he offered, rubbing his hands vigorously.

"Just cool it a bit, Jackie, okay?" Ray said.

Ray had invited Jackie to the session, so felt responsible for him. His style worked well for the Ten Pioneer Swingsters, for whom he played with Ray, but in the session context it tended to be intrusive.

"Relaxation won't do you any harm, dad," Philip added. His expression was hidden by the lenses of his dark glasses, but his relaxed tone indicated the satisfaction he felt at his own playing.

He turned to Fat: "So, where's Daddy today?"

"Lying down, Phil," Fat replied. Concern for his father's health, and pleasure with Philip's interest, competed in his face. "This week, as you would say, he has not been shit-'ot."

The musicians laughed.

Ray, impatient to start playing, blew a few notes. Then, without looking at him, said to Philip, "I feel like 'Summer Time', brother."

They both looked across at Jackie. "Relax, relax," Ray said.

***

Ray was in a musically productive period. In addition to the sessions at Fat's house, the Swingsters were playing regularly in Edendale, and he had a weekly gig at the Bombay Corner. It followed a two month barren patch after the death of his father. He had been forced to pawn his trumpet to help the family meet the funeral costs, but mourning and new family responsibilities would have curtailed his playing in any case. As the oldest son, he had guided the reorientation of the family and assumed responsibility for the home. He had filled this new role unquestioningly and with confidence. Like Fat Singh his identity was deeply rooted in his family, and in the home he had lived in all his life.

As a youth Ray had been given a battered trumpet by an uncle, and had taught himself the basic skills in a few months. Soon his abundant natural talent had been recognised by a local Marabi band which invited him to sit in at shebeen gigs. His youthfulness had provided a special attraction. He abandoned school for a job in the Native Police Band, where he had the opportunity to play a better instrument and learn to read music. The Band dissolved within two years, but by then Ray had exploited the opportunity to the full, and had saved enough to buy himself a reasonable trumpet.

A succession of jobs and musical dates had followed, until he was invited to join the Swingsters immediately after the War. The Swingsters played Marabi, American swing, marches, church music - whatever it took to secure a date and make money. They were music makers, not jazzmen. But one of the senior members, a relatively wealthy landowner and school teacher, was a great fan of American jazz. He had a large collection of records, mostly of the Chicago bands of the twenties and thirties. It was in his house that Ray had developed his passion for jazz. Initially seduced by the big bands of Basie and Lunceford, Ray's first idol, inevitably, had been Louis Armstrong. It was much later, in Fat Singh's house, that he heard recordings of Sweets Edison and Roy Eldridge, and so acquired the sound which Philip found complementary to his own. When Philip met him, he was, in Philip's words, "ripe for bop". But their meeting was cemented not so much by the shape of Ray's blowing as by the feeling which infused it. When he blew, he dug deep.

***

The jam sessions at Fat's house had been initiated by Ray, in response to Philip's interest in him and obvious respect for his playing. This was not a white man trying to do good by a black one - Philip was a jazzman whose own playing came before anything else, but who saw in Ray someone whose playing would extend his own. Ray was excited by the possibilities. Jazz, the music in which he expressed himself most readily, was a small part of the Swingsters' repertoire. Most of the time he blew what he had to, not what he wanted to. Collaboration with Philip promised to fill the gap.

It was almost a month after his first attempt that Philip had again visited Ray at the garage. This time he had arrived just before the final hooter, and caught Ray as he was leaving the yard. They had walked together to Ray's West Street bus stop. Both men wore heavy

The mountains which towered all around the hotel might not have existed. Both felt comfortable, as they would not have done outside in an environment without walls and drenched in sunlight.

"How are your London plans going?" Philip asked.

"On course." Faith folded her legs up under her, steadying herself against Philip's thigh.

She was wearing tight, black jeans which ended half way down her calves, and a chunky, wine red jersey. Red, half-moon shaped earrings hung from the ears exposed proudly by her short-cropped hair. Philip glanced at her as he expelled cigarette smoke through his nostrils. This chick is not pretty, he thought. Her face is too long, her nose too big. But her sexuality is electric, overt in every movement she makes.

"What about your mother?" he asked.

"C'mon Phil," she grinned, "It's not like you to be concerned about domestic matters." Her accent was very proper, with an almost Oxford intonation. The result of a mannered home environment and private school education.

"Mum will be fine. All her friends are here, and a couple of aunts. She loves the fucking society scene - bridge, church, tea parties, and all the other analgesics."

Philip grunted. "Sounds like fun."

Faith's thigh was pressing against his.

"You know, I don't think she even missed my father. She seemed to blossom after he died - became confident as she never was with him; bought her little hat shop with all the money he left her; got to do things she had never had time for."

Philip changed position so that his thigh pushed in under hers. "Did they get on with each other?" he asked.

She looked at him for a long time before answering. Her dark eyes, predominant in a face of prominent features, were sending many signals. "Outwardly they did. After all, he *was* a fucking gentleman. But he was hard, very hard. Not like you, Phil." She placed a hand on his shoulder. "Mannerless, hard outside, but soft inside."

"Christ," he said, and gulped the last of his brandy. "If only you knew."

***

Throughout the gig that night Philip was distracted. He played with a lot of emotion, but by his own standards he was all over the place. His thoughts were enthralled by what he knew would happen later. He was not conscious of having taken a decision - like an adolescent, he felt swept into a realm in which decisions were taken for him. Notions of betrayal, of cheating, were excluded from this realm; emotion, untrammelled by ideas, held sway.

In the early hours of the morning he went to Faith's room. No words passed between them until they had spent the powerful, inexorable physical force between them. After dipping in and out of sleep for a time, words came back to them.

"Are you thinking of Patty?" she asked.

"No."

They were lying naked in each other's arms beneath a pile of blankets. Two smooth seeds in a thick, woollen pod.

"You must never feel guilty, Phil. It had to be."

"Oh, Christ," he said. "It's easy to feel that now. But tomorrow? Next week?"

She pushed herself up onto an elbow and fumbled out a cigarette. She offered him one. He sat up, and they smoked in silence for a while.

"For a long time I felt guilty. All the time," she said.

"What do you mean? For committing adultery?"

"No. About myself." She brushed ash from one of her breasts. "As an adolescent I was always fighting with my father. God he was self-righteous. After one fight - I can't even remember what it was about - I decided that I hated him. No place for greys - everything had to be black or white. Anyway, I prayed that he would die."

"Tough cookie," Philip said.

"Well he did die, just a couple of months later. And for a long time I thought it was my fault. Jesus, I told myself that I didn't even believe in God, and anyway why would he listen to me? But the guilt still festered."

Turning to her, Philip kissed her ear fleetingly. "There's so much of you I don't know," he whispered.

She shook her head. "You know me, Phil."

Again ash fell on her breast. This time Philip brushed it off, then rolled over and pulled a joint from his shirt-pocket. He held it up to her. "Ever had one of these?"

Her tongue traced the line of her upper lip. "Once or twice. I didn't think it was very cool."

"Share it with me?"

She nodded. He lit up and passed it to her.

"I don't have a father," he said. "But I had an Italian."

She laughed out loud. "Christ, Phil, you're a hoot."

"No, seriously. Roberto was a prisoner of war in town. A great cat. He taught me a lot."

She gave him a serious nod.

"Better than anybody's father I've ever met or heard of," he continued. "But then, for all I know, maybe my parents were Italian and my feelings for Roberto were just a kind of blood response."

She giggled, then pulled him to her.

The pot was beginning to affect them. Both were aware of being drawn onto a different plane. Each felt the other to be an extension of themselves, and quivered to be properly joined.

***

With the others during the next morning and through lunch, Philip and Faith had to consciously avoid touching each other. They were sensitised to each other, aware of the other's every movement. The need to touch was a powerful, physical imperative. They secured the back seat of the Ford for the journey home, and conducted flippant conversation with Gladstone and Johnny, all the while at another level communicating only with each other. Philip tried not to think of home, more precisely of the act of walking in and greeting Patty. She will know immediately, he thought; it will be in my eyes, in the way I move. He looked at Faith, and was envious of her freedom. To do what she had to do, to go with whatever desire might possess her. Neither of them paid any attention to the panoramic distances stretching away from the vehicle on all sides - they might just as well have been in a basement closet.

Back in town, Philip asked Gladstone to drop them at the Town Hall.

"We'll pick up our things from your place a bit later," he said.

It was late afternoon, the warm colours - of brick, tar, bark and evergreen foliage - strange in the bitingly cold air. Gladstone leaned out as they walked away from the growling Ford:

"Do you two know what you're doing?"

Philip shrugged. "Who does, dad?"

They walked past the burnt orange walls of the Town Hall and into the Market Square.

"Fuck. I wanted to buy you flowers," he said. He gestured towards the row of flower stalls. They were boarded up, like a line of blind old women in colourful dresses.

She squeezed his hand. "Do you ever buy Patty flowers?"

"Sure," he answered, "mostly when I've treated her badly."

They stopped at Twiggy's Pie Cart and ordered coffees and a cowboy's breakfast - pie and beans. Faith was ravenous with the cavities pot fashions in a person.

"Do you think you can be in love with more than one person at the same time?" he asked.

"C'mon, Phil. Let's not talk about love."

"Regard it as a philosophical question," he replied.

She laughed. "I laugh a lot with you. I could fall in love with you just for that. No sure, I think you can. In fact, I think you must."

Philip pushed up his dark glasses with a thumb. "That's strong medicine, babe."

"But it's sensible, Phil. Not that I want to be sensible, you know, but if you think about it it's just common sense. It's absurd to think that one person can fulfil all your emotional and sexual needs. To stay alive you need a range of stimulation, diversity, even in your most intimate relationships. Maybe I'm just a promiscuous bitch, but that's what I believe."

Philip shook his head. "No, babe, you're making a lot of sense." He raised a hand to touch her, but withdrew it. "You must think I'm a real saphead for getting married, huh?"

Again the tinkling, infectious laugh. "I told you both that you were fools when you did it. Remember?"

It was dark by the time they reached the front gate of her mother's house. They embraced.

"Promise me something, Phil?"

He grunted.

"Leave this thing be. One fabulous weekend, nothing more. Soon I'll be gone, and you must think of Patty. She's a very special person."

He grasped her hands. "No promises. No guilt."

CHAPTER 14

Is it a peculiarity of bourgeois culture that most individuals shaped by it think of themselves as special, in some fundamental way more important than anyone else? Is it this notion which in turn spawns the assumption that everyone else must think of themselves in the same way? And which fuels the dream of recognition? From childhood Faith had been conscious of her unique importance and had felt destined for recognition on a stage bigger than that provided by Pietermaritzburg. Because she hadn't bothered to hide it, she had not been popular at school. It is one of the ironies of this culture that belief in one's importance must be hidden in the company of co-believers. Her irregular behaviour had fashioned, and been fashioned by, an irrepressible rebellion. Deliberate and catholic, it had led her into confrontation with every form of authority, from school prefects to God. Frequently destructive, it had at last found creative expression through her discovery of jazz.

In this music born of emotional extremes and lending itself to statements against any form of politeness, Faith had found both space for her frustrated imagination and a way out of the little town which she despised. Unlike Gladstone, she had not in her enthusiasm substituted jazz for her classical training. She had realised that the better trained her voice, the greater the options she kept open for the future. And so the apparent anomaly of the rebel who bucked all other discipline never missing singing practice; and the extraordinary sight of Faith Woolmer, dressed in white, singing solo roles in the school's annual Easter choral services.

Only twenty years old, Faith's views on sex and love, like all her views born of rebellion, had been fashioned by a broad experience. At their heart was rejection of the mode of thought which equates contradiction with error, which assumes or clings to absolutes, and in which all endings are either happy or sad. Instinctively she recognised that this mode is built on fear, dullness and blind hope, and is therefore an ideal means of exploitation. Passionately she embraced complexity, abandoning dreams of security for more tenuous rewards.

Her first lover, taken when she was still in school uniform, had been a doctor who shared a practice with the Woolmers' family doctor. He had been followed by others, usually older men bearing the allure of a father figure promising to blot out the image of her own father. Apart from a single still-born encounter during a drunken sequel to a gig, Philip was the first jazz musician with whom she had slept. Generally she found jazz musicians too juvenile to be attractive. He was also the first lover who was married to someone she knew. And she liked Patty. This was a new equation - not that it presented her with moral difficulties, for it did not, but it made her uncomfortable. The source of her concern was not the equation itself - the immemorial triangle - but the other people in it. She knew that the love which Philip and Patty shared - fresh, raw - could not accommodate her. And she cared enough for Philip not to want it destroyed.

***

It was the Sunday after the Drakensberg gig. The afternoon air was warm with the promise of spring. The sunlight, reflected by squadrons of plump cumulus clouds, was not the harsh winter light which bleached the sky of colour. It's illumination was soft, impregnating the earth's subtle hues. Philip, hands in pockets, descended the West Street hill and crossed the Msunduze River bridge. Someone more appreciative of the natural world might have imagined the arid earth straining for the first rains; felt the innumerable seeds pouched in its dryness awaiting transformation. He was thinking of Faith, absorbed by the hunger of his own body.

His sexual appetite, starved since Lauren's birth, had been awakened by the weekend with Faith. The tension of it had excited him all week, impelled him to break the barriers between him and Patty. They had made love each day, at unusual times for them, in the lightness of renewal. For both of them the pleasure had been exquisite, embellished by many small discoveries and surprises. But through it all Philip had been thinking of Faith.

He slowed his pace as he entered the crescent in which Faith lived. In the confusion of his thoughts he knew only that he had to see her. He stopped at the front gate, painted an obscenely bright silver. It was connected to the house by a paved path which split the front lawn into two perfect halves. The lawn's perimeters, marked by spacious, curved flower beds, were precisely defined. A neat, pretty garden of reason. Philip hesitated, as if unable to bring himself to touch the thick, silver paint. Suddenly he was baulked by the thought of what he might have to negotiate before he could be alone with Faith.

"Phil!"

She had been reclining in a chair on a patio half hidden by shrubs. He waited for her as she strode down the path. She was wearing a pair of shorts and a sleeveless top, her face hidden by the bulky lenses of her dark glasses. She grinned.

"Coming in; or just looking?" she said.

His hand grasped the gate. "Jesus. You look great."

She glanced back at the house. "Mum has a visitor. You're just in time for tea." She placed a hand on his. "For purposes of polite conversation you are a musician here to discuss musical arrangements with me."

Tea on the patio with the three women was an exercise in patience for Phil. More accurately, an exercise in disguised impatience. He successfully fended off the plate of cream scones, but was less successful in side-stepping the older women's interest in his religious background. They had attended a confirmation service together that morning, and were brimming with enthusiasm over what had been a very meaningful ceremony for them. Philip had to concede that he had been obliged to go through it as an adolescent at the Boys' Home.

"And tell me, Mr Maddox," Mrs Woolmer's friend asked, completing the demolition of her third scone, "are you still a Christian?"

"Well, Mrs Gaddy, I'm not sure," he replied. "I don't go to church, if that's what you mean."

"But do you believe in God?"

He looked at his persecutor. She had a smudge of cream on her upper lip. "Some days I do, some days I don't. It depends on how I've slept, what the weather's like, you know."

The two older women exchanged glances.

"Well!" Mrs Woolmer said.

Faith giggled as she led Philip into her bedroom. "So you suffer from religious rheumatism. It depends on the fucking weather!"

He looked around the room. For a moment he wondered if this was indeed her bedroom. Its walls were bare; the wooden floor had a single, modestly sized mat. It possessed no colour, no sense of the person who used it - it was a bare sleeping chamber, no more.

Philip closed the door and turned to her. "I..." The right words would not come. At that moment there were no right words; matching words to his jumbled feelings would have been a pointless exercise. He moved to her, and tentatively drew a hand through her hair. He fingered her ear, all the while searching her eyes. They embraced, a long, static embrace of sympathy rather than passion.

"Have you told Patty?" she asked.

He shook his head. Eyes closed, he drew in the smell of her, absorbed the feel of her breasts, shoulder, back and hands against him. He wished he would never have to utter another word.

From outside came the muffled voices of Mrs Woolmer and Mrs Gaddy. They were having a second cup of tea and finishing off the scones while they discussed the next church picnic.

***

At the flat Patty was stretched out crossways on the double-bed, one hand behind her head, the other palm down on the crocheted quilt she had knitted as a schoolgirl. She was drifting out of sleep, woken by the cries of two small boys playing with a tennis ball in the street below. Languidly she reached both hands down to her thighs, ran them over her stomach and up to her breasts. A faint smile played about her mouth. Her fingers weighed the fullness of the breasts, felt the nipples rise at the thought of Philip's hungry mouth upon them a few hours before. As urgent as Lauren's toothless little mouth. They had eaten lunch on the lounge floor, bent cross-legged over a clutch of plates, their heads ducking to touch each other in a gentle mating ritual. Afterwards, in a narrow space between plates, sewing work, and records, they had made love, slowly, both with eyes closed, almost as if in a dream. He had carried her to the bedroom, she already half asleep, and whispered that he would be back soon, he just had to fetch something from Johnny.

Lauren whimpered in the cot squeezed between the bed and the wall. Patty rolled over to look at the baby hunched awkwardly into one end of the cot. A tiny hand jerked up against the wooden bars, searching for the dummy. Patty slid off the bed to retrieve it and straighten the baby's limbs. She stayed to watch her settle into the last of her afternoon sleep. How that little body had resisted the spasms of her mother's weary body at birth! Patty's labour had stretched through an interminable afternoon and into evening, ending when the doctor was out, the delivery performed by two nurses watched by a thoroughly ravaged Philip.

She traced a finger down the finely crafted edge of the central bar. Without fanfare, almost embarrassed, Max had presented the cot to Patty days before Lauren's birth. Working from a photograph he had torn from a magazine, he had laboured in his workshop to produce something at once functional and beautiful. Patty smiled as she remembered his only visit to the hospital - so brief; a few uneasy words; an awkward refusal when offered Lauren to hold. But he had obviously been moved.

Patty stretched back onto the bed. She watched light reflected from somewhere outside dancing against the wall. She listened for the ball-players, but they had moved on or been called in for tea. Something in the conjunction of elements which formed the moment reminded her of a Sunday afternoon long past. It stood out as an aberration in the rigid Brennan routine. Max and Bertha had gone out, taking with them their older son. Was it a death, a christening, or some inexplicable visitation? And why had she been left at home to look after her baby brother? The answers, tantalisingly, lay beyond the reach of her memory. But the peace which had inhabited the house, her feeling of contentment, had been recorded indelibly. For once Max would not be drinking by himself next to his brandy cabinet; Bertha would not be sulking in the kitchen or stalking the passages. There would be no angry culmination. It had been a sublime intrusion of peace.

For as long as she could remember, Patty had been a mediator between the other members of her family, sometimes deflecting, sometimes absorbing, always sensitive to the destructive impulses carrying the family from one confrontation to the next. She had been thrust into maturity, learning as a child to accommodate others while deftly manipulating the bands which tied her to them. This pattern had also informed her relationships with boyfriends: always young, clumsy boys incapable of meeting her on equal terms. Until she met Philip. He had claimed her, laying down the terms of their meeting, yet providing her with the promise of what she yearned for - possession of another's deepest affection. For this was the object which had made of all her relationships a fruitless searching.

There were spasmodic movements from the cot, where Lauren was waking up. Patty leaned forward to watch her.

Philip had seduced her with his self-sufficiency which nevertheless allowed her a part of himself unreservedly. The contained, ultra cool jazzman contained in him a bewildered boy whom she could draw to herself. Like the night after his first session with Ray Gamede in Sobantu. She had found him in the lounge in the early hours of the morning. He had been staring into the darkened room, his legs, uncharacteristically, drawn up to his torso. She had stood behind him, her hands on his chest.

"How do we make sense of things?" he had said.

"Phil," she had whispered, and kissed his head.

"So many great things. Beauty. But so much shit." His shoulders had contracted as he fought back his tears.

A bewildered boy. How she cherished those inexplicable shafts which exposed him to her!

Lauren wailed her awareness of hunger. Her hands were clenched into angry fists. Patty paused to look at the tiny, impatient being who was completely hers, before scooping her up.

PART III

WINTER 1955

CHAPTER 15

I stretch out on the carpet, a pile of cushions propping up my head. At my right hand, bright brown in the chunky glass I lifted from some hotel, my first brandy of the day. Last night we played a great gig - one of those inexplicable comings together; everyone sharp, wailing without strain. Afterwards, deep into the morning, I dropped into the happy, refreshing sleep of the just. And I'm still feeling abnormally fresh, you know. At my feet, dressed all in white, an angelic pixie engrossed in serious business, Lauren crouches over a collection of coins and pieces of scooby-dooby wire. She mumbles an incomprehensible incantation as she breaks a pyramid of farthings and carefully places one of them with her pennies. Then she attempts, unsuccessfully, to balance a piece of red, white and blue wire on top of the column of pennies. She gives me a worried glance, holding up the intransigent little tricolour.

"Won't work, my Dad. Won't work."

I lean over, top the column with a florin, and settle the wire on it with a flourish.

"Shot!" she squeals, delight in her Brennan blue eyes.

We smile at each other, and I feel very cool.

Here should be the ingredients of a good day. But the sense of cool is fleeting, quenched by the thought of the afternoon to be spent with the Brennans. And because today is an occasion - the July Handicap, for Christ's sake - other relatives will be there as well. Talk about a fucking handicap!

I feel a tickling sensation on my hand - the whiskers of Cat, alias Mister Cool, our tortoise shell tom. His head hovers over the glass, his eyes dark, suspicious, then he jerks away and pads heavily over to Lauren. She is painstakingly unwinding the strands of a long piece of scooby-dooby wire. Cat pauses at her side, flops down on his back and raises an exploratory paw to the wire.

" 'Allo, Mister Cat," Lauren says very formally.

He hooks the wire out of her hand, and half rolls to watch it fall beyond their reach. His legs are splayed, revealing the thick winter fur of his white stomach.

Lauren giggles. "Mister Cat funny." She looks up at me. "My Dad, Mister Cat funny."

I give her a wink. "Stroke him, Lollipop; like Dad taught you."

He came to us in the summer, from the shopyards below, at the time when Lauren was in quarantine for measles. As though he had planned it that way, you know. I had taken a few days off work to give Patty a hand in the darkened flat. It turned out to be a special time for me - it was then, in a scene transformed by Lauren's spotted body, the drawn curtains, the advent of Cat, that I really started relating to Lauren. After a false start on the first morning. I was trying to interest her in the illustrations in one of my old William books, but she wanted her grandmother: "Where Gaga? Where Gaga?" she had repeated over and over. Frustrated, I eventually said: "Gaga's in my hip pocket." That upset the hell out of her. But we made up, and for the rest of the time gave each other a kick exploring all the little things that more than fill a child's day. She takes nothing for granted; everything is a potential happening, even routine things like meals and bath times. Christ, if we could live like that all our lives!

I finish my brandy and push myself up from the floor. "Lolly, Dad's going to the toilet. You look after things here, okay?"

She grunts, something she's picked up from me, but doesn't look up. Too busy sorting out her dough, like some weird little shopkeeper.

Patty will be ready to go soon, and I need a joint before taking on the nuthouse. In the yellow retreat I pause before the medicine chest, another of the growing number of creations coming out of Max's workshop. The mirror clipped to its door reflects my pale dial, which sports the goatee I still haven't got used to - Patty hates this latest attempt to modify my image, but I kind of dig its suggestion of maturity.

I pull a joint from the old Disprin box, take a pew on the throne, and light up. Just a couple of drags and I begin to relax. Marilyn

Monroe, my latest addition to the door, gazes down at me from a scene in that great movie 'Bus Stop'. I wait for the familiar contentment to inhabit me, but it won't come. Hovering behind Monroe is an image of Ray's eyes. In vain I try to blink them away. They are still burning his disappointment, as they did two weeks ago after that disastrous gig. I had had a bad day, and in an attempt to get back in tune really bombed out on pot. I was awful. Ray came up to me afterwards - I can't remember what he said, but the message in his eyes was enough.

Bombing out is an occupational hazard. Most of the time it is unpredictable, and sometimes I *let* it happen through bloody-mindedness. It isn't cool, you know, and I hate it. Another thing I'm beginning to hate about pot is the way I drift out of Lauren's reach when I'm stoned. Well, out of reach of anybody who isn't also stoned. Which is precisely why I'm using it now. This must all sound pretty contradictory. Anyway, suddenly Marilyn Monroe is sharp, untroubled by any images created by my fear. I am easing into the peacefulness which only pot can give me. A luxurious sense of cool.

Monroe collapses into herself and disappears as the door opens. For a moment Lauren stands motionless, a hand clutching the door, as she assesses her discovery, weighs up significances.

"My Dad poo?"

I shake my head. "Just meditating, kiddo."

She gabbles in response, but seems satisfied.

" 'Olly need poo," she says, pulling at her woollen suit.

I unclothe her and put her on the pot she has only recently mastered. She chatters to me and herself, pausing only to bend forward and scrutinise each stool as it hits the bottom of the pot. She hasn't inherited my stubborn bowels. I am wiping her backside, counting each wipe for her to repeat triumphantly, when Patty walks in.

"Phil, you're not going like that," she says.

By 'that' she means the uniformly black clothing I'm wearing. A number of sarcastic responses suggest themselves, but I stick to simplicity:

"Sure," I say.

***

I am sitting on the back verandah of 89 Woodhouse Road - 'Pandokkie', according to the polished copper plaque Max has screwed to the front door. The horse race is over, the huddle around the radiogram has dispersed, and I have fetched up on a chair to have my hair cut.

"Keep still, Philip," Bertha tells me as she wields her massive pair of scissors about my ears.

This operation I dig. It calms my nerves, and I feel closer to Bertha than at any other time. Relatively speaking, of course. I sit quietly, swathed in a sheet, like an obscene ice cream cone topped by an old, black cherry. Below us in the back yard I can see Max working on the Austin with one of his sons; the other son is playing with cousins in a loquat tree; and Lauren, attended by an ugly girl of indeterminate filiation, is playing on a swing. Sitting in front of her, occasionally barking with aged voice, is Patty's old spaniel, Scamp.

"Let me cut it off," Bertha says.

Like Patty, she doesn't dig my goatee. I shake my head.

"Keep still." And then a final, tour de force of persuasion: "It makes you look like an Afrikaner. It's gratuitous."

"Well," I mumble, aiming benignly at the word I think she was after, "at least it's not grotesque."

Which cannot be said of the proceedings which attended the horse race. Max is passionate about nags, and as with everything he does, he expresses it with a precision and thoroughness which really knocks me out. In one of the set of notebooks he keeps in his brandy cabinet he records the form of every bloody nag in the southern hemisphere. In another he enters details of all his bets - at any time he can tell you exactly what his winnings, or losings, have been in the last month, year, ten years, whatever. For the July Handicap he prepares a card for each nag - on which he pastes a newspaper photograph and inscribes in his neat hand all the details which might interest a punter. Those who have gathered at 89 draw numbers from his father's old police hat, and are ceremonially handed matching cards. Each adult places half a crown in the kitty, the commentary is listened to, the winner handed the kitty and congratulated by Max, and finally we escape to swings or hair cuts. To be fair, some of us enjoyed it. Patty did - after all, she *did* win - and so did the younger kids.

"Philip, I hope you don't think I'm interfering now," Bertha introduces a decisive act of interference.

My stomach rumbles in protest at the glob of overcooked meat resisting its best digestive endeavours.

"Don't you think you should spend less time on your jazz hobby? Especially now that you must be thinking of a second child."

I wonder what she would do with that big fucking pair of scissors if I gave her the answer straining at my lips. I make a sound expressing something between despair and confusion to give me more time to consider consequences.

"What's that?" she asks, the scissors marching across my fringe.

Jesus. Talk about feeling close to her! Too fucking close. I laugh a pathetic little laugh.

"Keep still!"

Inspiration comes at last. "It's something to think about," I say.

And then I am saved by Bertha's brother-in-law; tall, vulture-like Wayde Silver. He wanders out onto the verandah, chewing on a scrap of leftovers he has scavenged from the kitchen. His avaricious eyes cast about as his mouth processes what to most humans would be inedible.

"Still hungry, Wayde?" Bertha asks.

Even for Bertha a rhetorical question. Wayde Silver is *always* hungry.

"Mmmm," he replies, his tongue probing his cheeks for any morsel which has still escaped the big plunge.

I am dismissed by Bertha, the decisive shaking of the sheet a washing of hands. Wayde Silver fields me, his small talk failing to reassure me that he is not considering how tasty I would be after a few hours roasting on a spit. We stroll over to the Austin, me all the while casting about for a way of escape.

"Ah, Max, a new wrench," he observes.

Wayde Silver towers over Max, who is manipulating the wrench in the depths of the Austin's engine. Tools, like food, glasses, and any other fucking thing which isn't nailed down, are irresistible to Wayde Silver. Max knows this, which is why he has applied a daub of green paint to each of his tools. Wayde Silver's eyes, shameless, have noticed that the wrench is unadorned.

"My Dad! My Dad!"

Lauren has seen me from the swing, and comes running towards us with a commitment that invites calamity. Scamp trots behind her, less dangerously, his ears flapping beside his front paws. She launches herself at me, a bundle of innocence, and I draw her to me. I breathe in the smell of her - the only smell of life at this fucking funeral.

"Mommy winned!" she says triumphantly, as if for the first time.

"Isn't Mommy clever?" I respond. And then, inspiration really flowing, "Shall we take Scamp for a walk?"

She grunts a qualified agreement, and we move off to the bottom of the yard. We pass the ugly girl sitting listlessly on the swing.

"My horse never wins, Uncle Philip," she whines.

"You should complain," I reply. "Mine is still running."

We can still hear her giggling as we make our way past the compost heaps and into the wild veld.

CHAPTER 16

The kitchen was warm with the soft light of a winter afternoon. Walls, furniture, and all the paraphernalia required to make food edible and attractive, their metal or white-painted surfaces harsh under electric lighting, seemed almost natural in the gathering dusk. As if in an aqueous medium, Patty moved from stove, to sink, to sideboard, her thoughts gliding in and out of form. Noises from outside, Lauren's occasional shouts from the lounge, were vibrations from almost forgotten dreams. Effortlessly she inhabited a peace which Philip - through intense creativity or the seduction of pot - found only rarely.

With a clatter of limbs and voices, Lauren and Philip entered the tiny room. As Philip embraced her from behind, Patty looked up from the onion she was dicing with relaxed but sure strokes. His hands crossed beneath her apron to cup her breasts; his mouth explored her neck.

"Hello, silent siren of mine," he whispered.

Lauren joined the embrace, grasping Patty's knees.

"*My* Mommy," she asserted.

Patty and Philip had put behind them the long period of alienation which followed his disclosure of his relationship with Faith. The process, for both of them a painful assimilation of destructive emotions and feelings, had forged a new orientation to their relationship - deeply rooted in which, and informing the cycles of intimacy and distance, was a reinforced mutual recognition of each's irrevocable otherness. Patty had realised that her dream of two halves meeting to make a whole would never have substance.

Who can know the fragile dynamics of sexual love? How mysterious the feeling of closeness lovers experience; it comes, it goes, responsive to diverse and complex forces. Like the opening and closing of a butterfly's wings.

"Need outside, Mommy; outside." Lauren was pulling impatiently at Patty's dress.

By outside Lauren meant the miniature park tucked behind the Deeds Office nearly a block away. Patty often walked her there to escape the confines of the flat.

"It's too late, little one," Patty said. "You must have your bath."

Philip gathered Lauren up and made for the bathroom. He paused at the kitchen door.

"God, honey, tonight is going to be a disaster," he said.

Patty shook her head, something between a smile and a grimace about her mouth.

Dinner parties were anathema to Philip - he despised their formalities and resented the absence of escape routes from boring conversations. They made him nervous. Patty had secured his consent to this one only after months of persuasion - she wanted to meet the wives of Fat and Ray, and she wanted to do it properly.

"For Chrissakes, honey, these babes are in different worlds to us," Philip had protested. "Neither of them digs jazz nor understands where the fuck we're at; and Ray's wife can hardly speak English. The whole scene would be pretentious. Believe me."

Patty had ruffled his hair, something he hated, then smoothed it as she replied: "How typically male you are, Philip. Just because you relate to Fat and Ray in a tiny world where only music is important, you assume the women have nothing in common."

***

Philip and Ray had forged a musical collaboration that was relaxed but in which the edge of creative tension was ever present. Philip's use of pot, the only source of real dissonance between them, ebbed and flowed primarily with the energies of this relationship. For a while the jam sessions at Fat's had been its fulcrum, but these had ended after one was interrupted by policemen. It had been a Saturday afternoon overtaken unnoticed by evening. Ray had brought an alto saxophonist from the Swingsters with him, and the three hornmen had found a groove in which their wailing threatened a realisation of perpetual motion. The police, summoned by irate neighbours, jumped them violently out of their groove. The constable in charge took up a position in the centre of the room, and glared around him.

"So," he said, folding his arms and exchanging a knowing look with his most senior subordinate, "you boys are having a good time."

"A practice session, sir," Fat responded. "They are all respectable jazz musicians."

"Shut up, coolie," the important constable hissed. "Just because you live in a white area you think you're not a hooligan. But you forget not to act like a hooligan."

He pulled a notebook out of one of his many pockets. "This," he prodded it with a shapeless forefinger, "is my book of hooligans. Names and addresses."

With the assistance of his most senior subordinate, he took down all their names and addresses.

"And tell me, Mr Philip Maddox," he said after painstakingly recording Philip's details, "what do you want with kaffirs and coolies?"

Philip eased out a cigarette. He paused before lighting it. "You have a problem, dad," he said, smiling sweetly at him.

Philip's remark crystallised the important constable's problem for him. He instructed two of his own hooligans to take Philip outside, where they searched him and his Morris Minor.

"This time you're lucky, Mr Philip Maddox," the important constable said after the searches. "You carry on interfering with them," he jerked a thumb at Fat's house, "and it's only a matter of time before you get into trouble."

One of the hooligans threw him against the Morris, and they left in a chorus of polished shoes. Philip leaned back, breathing heavily and thanking somebody that he hadn't brought any joints with him.

This experience, a minor ripple on the surface for Philip, had completely unnerved Fat. He lived in hope that the Group Areas Act, passed in 1950, would never be applied in Pietermaritzburg; and he hoped that the antagonism of his white neighbours would dissipate. Terminating the jam sessions was a way of pushing back the uniformed servants of the state and protecting the space in which he kindled his hope.

It was shortly after this that Ray had stopped off at the Maddox's flat after work for the first time. Soon it had become a habit which filled the gap left by the sessions. Seldom accepting a drink, coming never more than once in a week, he would appear off the street, fedora in hand, to listen to records and talk music. Although limited, the bond which developed between the two men was close - precisely because neither was consciously building a friendship nor interested in getting to know the other. Their connection was a shared passion for jazz, further contiguity happening incidentally.

Gladstone's undertaking to invite Ray to play with the Quintet had borne fruit in the occasional gig at appropriate venues like The Blue Moon and the Cygnet Theatre. Ray fitted in well, his trumpet, increasingly shaped by his exposure to bop, filling space up front and enriching the band's sound. Fat ensured other opportunities for the two men to play together - at the Bombay Corner, and at the Naaz Cinema in Durban. And on two occasions Ray had arranged for Philip to sit in with the Swingsters at gigs in Edendale. These had been interesting but unfulfilling experiences for Philip. He went through the motions, inhibited by the Swingsters' township sound and tight reign on improvisation.

It was after the second gig in Edendale that Philip had paid his only visit to Ray's home. The Gamedes lived in a house close to the one tarred road in the township, the main road running through the greater Edendale valley into Pietermaritzburg. The modest brick house, without electricity or telephone, was situated at the front of a substantial plot. Tenants' dwellings, a patchwork of brick, stone, mud, wood and corrugated iron, stretched down one side, encroaching on what was once a large vegetable garden.

Philip had felt uncomfortable in the crowded sitting room. The chairs and beds around its perimeter were all occupied by adults, the floor by a gaggle of children - gathered to welcome the *umlungu*, the white man, from town. This reception, for Philip an intimidating meeting with a township Argus, was not of Ray's making - his mother had insisted on it. A large woman with formidable bosom and husky, male voice, she occupied a chair alongside Philip. With Ray as interpreter, she conducted polite conversation with him while Ray's wife - silent, gaze averted - served them tea and biscuits. A deadly combination, reflected by the strain in Ray's eyes and Philip's chain of cigarettes.

It had been an unnerving experience for Philip. Ray in his own home was not the man Philip had got to know, not the musician with whom he generated intimate communion. It had been like having a known space transformed by alien dimensions. Philip's response was unequivocal. He saw no point in attempting to engage a part of Ray which instinctively he felt to be impenetrable. Just as he had no desire to disclose more than a small part of himself to Ray.

***

By the main course the dinner party had built up momentum. Fat's wife was hitting it off with Patty in a tumble of talk about children, food and clothes. Another centre of gravity, working at a more leisurely pace, drew the men together. Ray had made some excuse for his wife.

"I have what could be an exciting proposal to make," Fat said, leaning forward. The glow of the candle in front of him cast highlights about his round cheeks. "It is my responsibility to provide musicians for a big Liberal Party social taking place soon." His hands, like cogs in a machine, were rocking rhythmically together.

Fat's wife turned from Patty. "Ronald has joined the Liberal Party, you know. We're all very proud of him. He's on the City Central branch committee."

Fat grinned boyishly. "That is not the point, Doreen. The committee wants a jazz band, and I know the best jazz musicians in town." He pointed across the table at Philip and Ray.

Response was slow in coming. Eventually Philip spoke: "I suppose they want a nice range of skin colour."

"Phil." Patty spoke softly, without intonation.

Fat gulped water from his glass.

Undeterred, Philip pursued him. "I'm right, huh?"

"In the Liberal Party race is not an issue," Fat's wife said sharply.

Fat was fingering his glass with both hands. He looked up at Philip. "Actually, I was hoping we could make it into a reunion of the jam sessions. James du Bois has agreed to play."

Philip pulled at his goatee, then smiled. "But not Jackie, I hope?"

Fat grasped at his words. "So you'll play, Phil?"

"Sure, as long as the dough's good."

"And you, Ray?" Fat's hands had left the glass and found each other beneath the candle.

Ray leant forward, his gaze fixed on the candle's flame. It drew an almost purple glow from his skin.

"It depends, Fat," he said. "I must talk to my family, you know, and the Swingsters." He ducked his head and pushed a forefinger into his widow's peak.

The Liberal Party's recent withdrawal from the Congress of the People had outraged many residents of Edendale. One of Ray's brothers, a factory worker, was a member of the African National Congress. For Ray there was no decision to be made.

A long silence ensued. The mood was captured by the sensual voice of June Christie, inhabiting the room from Philip's outsized loudspeakers. She was singing a down tempo blues number.

"What a heavenly voice," Patty said.

As if responding to a cue, Philip spoke: "Fat, what do you think of the Natal separatists?"

Ever since his absurd experience with Peter Collins, he had maintained a slight interest in their fortunes.

"Crazy people," Fat replied. "Crazy."

"Don't you think that any opposition to the Government, however crazy, is a good thing?" Patty asked. She looked around the table for affirmation.

It was Ray who responded. He shook his head, half laugh, half grunt expressing his dissent.

"Ray?" Patty prompted.

"No; for me it is much doing about nothing. It is only when the people are angry enough that a real opposition can force change. And when that time comes it won't be them, or the Liberals, who will lead us - it will be the workers and the Congress."

This was the first political statement any of them had ever heard Ray make.

***

In the hour before midnight, the townscape etched by the light of the winter moon, Philip walked the others down to Fat's car. The new Plymouth was parked behind Philip's Morris Minor.

"Jeeze, dad, this thing will give my heap an inferiority complex," Philip said.

"No, Phil," Fat responded, "cars have something people will never learn - peaceful co-existence."

His wife laughed out loud.

Ray held Philip's hand as they parted. "Phil, there is something to be said. I have a chance to go to Joburg."

"Yeah? Someone give you a date?"

"Well, you could say it. They want me permanently."

Philip was stunned.   Ray, more than anyone else, seemed entrenched in Pietermaritzburg.

"I want it," Ray continued.   "There are others who must also say; but Phil, I really want it."

For a moment the two men looked at each other.   Then Philip grasped Ray's shoulder with his other hand.

"That's cool, dad. Take it."

He watched the Plymouth ease out from the kerb, stop at the robots, and disappear into Church Street. The night was still. Hands in pockets, he strolled across the street to get a better view of the moon. It shed its soft light from a star-filled sky.

"An empty smoke ring that has gone with the wind," he sang roughly to himself. A line from one of Faith's favourite numbers.

CHAPTER 17

It was a long Monday for Philip. Any day spent out on a job with his boss was a long one. The combination of unrelenting sunlight and mutual hostility worked on his nerves like a rhythm section which could not swing. And Ray's words the previous night had nudged him against a cliff edge - the time had come, and it had been a long time coming, to break the pattern his life had assumed in the last two years. Screened by his dark glasses and an array of grunts, Philip somehow made it through to five o'clock.

"I'd see a doctor if I were you, Maddox," his boss said as he dropped Philip off at the workshop.

"Yeah, dad. And if I were you, I'd see a magician."

***

That night Philip and Patty made important decisions. After supper Philip read Lauren a story - more precisely, invented tales around illustrations in a book - then put her down. She made several sorties to the lounge before staying put. Promotion from the cot to a bed had its excitements. Eventually alone, Philip and Patty took up their familiar positions on the lounge floor. On the turntable Ella Fitzgerald hummed the blues.

"Honey, I can't take the workshop anymore," Philip said, pushing his hand through the hair he had allowed to grow into a bush which sprang from his head.

"Then leave."

"That simple, huh?" Philip held his cigarette between thumb and forefinger, a habit he had picked up from smoking joints.

Patty placed a cigarette in her mouth and raised the candle she had placed between them to it. She took two shallow puffs. "I'm ready to go back to the office. It could work out well."

He watched her, a frown focused between his eyebrows. He gauged the lower, unattractive part of her face - pointed chin, small mouth, narrow nose - before engaging her eyes. They dominated the other features by their large surfaces and suggestion of depth. Their hue was the subtle blue of a clear sky at dusk.

Philip looked down, ostensibly for the ashtray. "What about Lauren?"

"I can get her into a nursery school for the mornings. Mom could look after her in the afternoons."

They talked at length about the options. Philip was dead against Lauren spending so much time with Bertha. The compromise was for him to manage domestic affairs in the afternoons.

"It would be good for you, Phil," Patty said. "And for Lauren."

At first he baulked at the idea. This was the antithesis of cool; and musically he would be loading the dice against himself. But Patty was persuasive. Besides being the only practical alternative in the circumstances, it offered him a framework possessing an inherent balance.

"Jesus, honey," he said. "I dig what you're saying, but in jazz, you know, balance can be death."

She moved the candle aside and manoeuvred herself closer to him.

"I mean, Greasy Aubrey was balanced."

She laughed. "But he wasn't an artist, Phil. And, to quote you, the saphead hadn't a clue what jazz was about."

***

It was after midnight. Philip had long tired of serving the turntable. They lay in each other's arms, between the candle's flicker and the warm glow of their small heater. His hand had worked its way beneath her pullover and found the soft contours of her breasts.

"Will you make me a big promise?" she said.

He buried his face in her hair.

"Not to smoke pot when you're with Lauren."

"Sure, babe." His mouth was moist against her ear. "I'd decided to give it up anyway," he lied.

Since the bad gig with Ray he had been thinking about the possibility.

Patty reached a hand up to his face. "How about a hot bath?"

***

Sleep did not come easily to Philip. There was a lot to think about. He lay on his back; Patty, like a small animal, huddled up against him. He wondered how it was that for so long he had regarded her as a fetter. Surely she hadn't changed? But the sense of being tied down, stagnating, had been overwhelming. Pot had offered a means of transcending it. So had Faith.

He remembered how he had decided not to tell her about Faith. Ironically it had been a good time for them, the renewed vitality injected into their relationship by his awakening with Faith fashioning a sustained closeness. And then he had received the letter from London.

It had arrived at work, a message from what was already his past. Faith was a dangerous experience, an idea, dismissed from his present without being assimilated. He had put the letter in his pocket, borne it with him through the morning, an ominous presence, until he could escape to a coffee shop at lunch time. There he had contemplated throwing it away unread. But that had not really been an option.

"Dear Phil

For a long time 'Dear Phil' stared back at me from an otherwise blank page. Not even the old 'How are you? I am fine' routine would work, because I am not so fine.

Do I still have a place in your thoughts? Or have you blown us away through that magnificent horn of yours? (Fuck, how this must bore you. No more questions, I promise.)

I miss you Phil. Not only since I arrived in London. It was worse in those last couple of months in PMB, when you were as close as the telephone.

Part of me thinks this letter is a bad idea. It carries so much pain, and will surely be a Pandora's box for you. But I owe you, Phil.

We were careless when we fucked. Remember? And I fell pregnant.

Phil, are you still there?

Some days, particularly those relentlessly grey London days after Christmas, I thought it was wrong for me to take a decision for both of us. In the end there seemed to be no alternative. I decided on an abortion.

That was the hard part. The rest has been frighteningly easy. Mother has money and wealthy relatives here with contacts.

So, here I am in this very nice clinic almost on the banks of the Thames. From my window I can see grass, trees, the river, and in the distance, Tower Bridge. They - the doctor, in his dark suit and darker tie, and the nurses in their blue and white striped dresses - care for me. And the life - because that is what it was Phil - has been taken out of me.

It was the right decision. I have no doubts, no regrets. But I am discovering that it was too fucking big to have taken without you. Christ. What I would give to feel your arms around me now.

I suppose it's obvious I'm feeling pretty fragile. But don't worry about me - I'm a survivor.

Surviving for what, though?

This morning I sat at my window, and looked down into the street that runs behind the clinic. A group of women, wearing dull clothes but each carrying a brightly-coloured brolly, crossed below me. They broke into a chorus of giggles and shrieks when a car bore down on them at speed. One sprinted, one or two trotted, and the rest, maintaining decorum, just quickened their pace. Somehow for

me the image was a symbol of what life is
about - a brief flurry between pavements.

It would be great if you found time in
your flurry to write to me. I haven't been
able to blow you out of my thoughts. Not
yet.

     With love,
      Faith"

In a daze he had sat in the coffee shop well past the end of his
lunch break. He had not re-read the letter. That was unnecessary.

For almost a week he had retreated into a pot-sustained inward
journey. Some way into the trip he had destroyed the letter, still not
re-read, and written a long one of his own in reply. It was a
rambling, incoherent expression of his confusion. Her letter had
resurrected his feelings for her, overturning the emotional and
intellectual processes which had secured for him the alienation of their
shared experience. He repeatedly slipped into the third person in a
subconscious denial of responsibility. On the abortion his words were
those of a reluctant equivocator. Of *course* she had made the right
decision; it was what he would have wanted. Anyway, it was rightly
her decision. Expressions of empathy, artificial, clumsy, barely
disguised his relief that she had not involved him in it, and that she
had made the decision she had. And genuine concern was weighted
by fear that she would fail to assimilate it without having to draw him
into the process. Words of affirmation and encouragement were
undermined by his assertion that yes, after all, life was but a ball of
shit. Everything he wrote obscured the truth he would not confront: I
care for you, love you, but for Christ's sake don't complicate my life
any more than you have.

Ironically, having sent the letter he had discovered that he could
not avoid complications. Faith and circumstance had smoothed the
way before him, but the combination made no impression on his
imagination. Currents of guilt haunted him; those he succeeded in
dismissing in his waking hours returned to torment his sleep. Finally,
emotionally drained, and in an attempt to appease these stubborn
currents, he had told Patty about his affair with Faith. He stopped
short of the pregnancy, and of the letters.

It had been a hot summer evening. The air had been close, heavy with moisture. They sat in the passage to catch any breeze which the opened front door would admit. Philip put down the book he had been staring at, and unburdened himself. It was not premeditated. He simply had to tell the story. For a long time after he had finished, Patty, arms hugging her shoulders despite the heat, sat in silence. Then she got up and walked to the front door. When eventually she spoke, she seemed to address the comfortless night she had been staring into:

"You know what really gets me, Philip? Your dishonesty." She caught a sob. "Why didn't you tell me?"

CHAPTER 18

Gladstone placed the record on the turntable with deft movements of his pale, slender hands. He stepped back as a forest of hiss and crackle sprang into the room from two coffin-like loudspeaker cabinets. It overwhelmed the thin sound of the Quintet, already well into a number, which eventually emerged. They had made the recording in 1952, Bertie Smit cutting onto shellac disc extracts from tapes of a practice session.

Behind Gladstone, seated sideways on a chair, Philip marked the beat with movements of his head. He was here at Gladstone's invitation, to listen to records before they made the Liberal Party date.

The character of the large bedroom had not changed since the years in which it had couched their shared adolescent explorations. There was more sound-reproduction equipment, more records and books, but the furnishing, the piano, the chaotic configuration, remained the same. Mother's mark was just evident - in the vase of flowers on the window-sill, and in the neat pile of ironed clothes on the bed.

With a grin, Gladstone turned to Philip in the silence which marked the groove's end: "You can just hear us. But even then we were worth listening to, huh?"

Philip nodded, then stroked his cheeks. They were unshaven, a vague statement of his feelings about the Liberal Party.

"We haven't moved, dad," he said.

Gladstone ducked his head, and awkwardly turned back to his records. He selected one he had bought recently, a recording in the long playing $33^{1}/_{3}$ rpm format of the Stan Getz Quintet in concert. He flipped the lighter vinyl disc onto the newer of his two turntables, lowered the arm, then shuffled over to the bed. There he paused, his back to Philip.

The muted, disconnected sounds of the rhythm section warming up died into a sharp round of applause. And suddenly Duke Ellington was speaking in relaxed, seductive tones:

"Thank you. Ladies and gentlemen, I have been given the very happy privilege

"Sure don't." James took a long drag. "But they mean well, right? And a lot of the things they say sure as hell need saying."

Philip grunted.

They finished their smokes in silence.

"So, what's your scene, dad?" Philip asked.

"Nothing scintillating, you know. Odds and ends."

"What are you doing for dough?"

"Same as always - signwriting with my brother. Like he's sharp, right, so the business is going well."

James rented a room from his brother in Indian town. Although the state had decreed the Du Bois' to be white, they preferred to remain in the mixed race area which reminded them of Mauritius.

Philip pulled at his goatee. "You open to possibilities? I mean a regular position someplace."

It was no more than a notion drifting through his brain.

"Like wow, dad." James grinned. "Let me hear yah talkin' to me."

***

Nuptial duty rather than political persuasion had brought Peter Collins to the party. His wife of just over a year was an active Liberal and determined enough to bend his will in most matters. So he bore his mild irritation with the music and discomfort at the presence of well dressed blacks with stiff upper lip. Besides, he was able to ease his passage by drawing about him several acquaintances from his social and professional circles.

He had hoped to avoid talking to Philip, but during a break in sets after the speeches they bumped into one another at the drinks table. Etiquette demanded that he introduce Philip to his wife. After the customary pleasantries, before Philip could articulate a suitable excuse for leaving, she told him how much she enjoyed his playing.

Philip inclined his head slightly. "You are gracious," he said. He was a little drunk.

She leant towards him, her wine glass held below her chin. "You are obviously committed to music."

Philip could find no response. He concentrated on not allowing his gaze to fall to the generous bosom which her low cut dress drew attention to.

"Commitment," she continued, "is a very attractive quality."

"I guess so," he said, and glanced at Peter, who was looking around the room. "So, Peter, are you still committed to the fight for freedom?"

"Certainly, old man."

After the collapse of the Defenders of the Constitution in the wake of the 1953 election, Peter had joined the newly established Union Federal Party. Based largely in Natal, it continued the anti-republican and Natal separatist traditions in the province. Peter was one of the architects of its Anti-Republican Leagues, organisations designed to secure popular support amongst the white electorate for the Union Federal Party.

"You know, it's a great pity that for you guys freedom has a white skin."

Peter glanced quickly around him. The pale skin of his neck was flushed. "You are quite wrong," he said. "We have a deep concern for the interests of the natives, and enjoy very good relations with their leaders. You have only to look at the record of Heaton Nicholls to see that." He lowered his voice. "We are in Africa, old man. The white man ignores it's realities at his peril."

Philip tried to smother a sneer in his brandy. Then he spoke with studied seriousness. "I don't exactly follow the career of Heaton Nicholls, but I know enough to know that he wouldn't recognise reality if it raped him in a public place."

For a moment Peter stared at him incredulously. "Excuse me," he said turning to his wife, "shall we move on?"

"I'll join you in a moment, dear."

As Peter limped away Philip mumbled an apology. "We always grated each other, you know."

"No need to apologise, I assure you. In essence what you say is right."

A large jewel glinted above her cleavage. It trembled as she moved closer to him.

"You support the Liberal Party then?" she asked.

"Christ, no!"

She smiled. "But surely ..."

"Listen, I don't dig politics, period." Philip's empty glass and her cleavage were beginning to make him feel nervous.

"Ah, I think I understand. You sympathise with our ideals though?"

He pulled viciously at his goatee. "I'm pretty ignorant, you know, but certain things here give me the shits." He gestured at the crowd around them. "This scene stinks of paternalism." For the first time an earnestness crept into his tone. "It doesn't break through the chains of protected privilege."

She touched her neck, fingered the chain, grasped the jewel. "But that is precisely what we're trying to do."

"Yeah, sure," he said, staring into his glass.

CHAPTER 19

This is an interlude in my daily routine when being cool is as accessible as a bank overdraft. I stand on the pavement outside the Three Oaks Nursery School waiting for the kids to explode from the front gate at one after midday. Part of a gaggle of mothers and maids, I am conspicuous not so much by my sex as by my studied silence. I glare morosely at anyone who looks like wanting to strike up a conversation with me. I'm not unfriendly by nature, you know, but the thought of having to explain myself kills me. Christ, this is as bad as the confirmation classes I was forced to attend when I was a kid in the Boys' Home.

At last the gate is opened by the vice-principal, Mrs Wilby, and the explosion happens. Lauren, her miniature brown suitcase held tightly in both hands, is shouting an inaudible greeting. After only four weeks at the school, she already digs the place the most. I claim her from the scrum, and hoist her into my arms, but before I can plunge away I am confronted by Mrs Wilby.

"Ah, Mr Maddox, I've been wanting to meet you."

She leers at me through horn-rimmed spectacles. Christ. A formidable sight, this tall babe in woollen dress and stockings, her hand thrust out at me. I take it, and smack a smile on my dial.

"You are what one might call an unusual parent, Mr Maddox. Tell me, what do you do for a living?"

She's the kind of babe you can't picture in bed, but who leaves you with the suspicion that she really takes off when she's there.

"I'm a musician," I mumble apologetically.

"Ah." She smiles at Lauren, who is pressing her suitcase into my chest impatiently. "That explains little Lauren's creativity."

I want to say something rude, but the school has bent rules to admit Lauren before she is three years old, so I swallow it.

"Well, nice talking to you," I say as the suitcase rears up at my nose. "I think we must blow."

Back at the flat I try to interest Lauren in an afternoon kip, but she wants to get out. There is no pattern to our afternoons together - most days she has a kip, some days she's happy to play in the flat while I read or listen to music, and then there are the times when all she wants is outside.

So after grabbing myself a sandwich, I dunk her in the pushchair and we head for Alexandra Park. Avoiding unnecessary exposure to sunshine and greenery has been a constant in my life, but Lauren's passion for both is beginning to work changes. We pass Grey's Hospital and descend the steep slope to the river. At Macfarlane's Bridge I hoist her out the chair to collect pebbles before we negotiate the wood and iron arch. When we reach the arch's high point she pushes the pebbles through the iron bars one at a time. She squeals delightedly as each one hits the water far below.

Back in the chair on the other side, she catches sight of the Pavilion, a Victorian grandstand which dominates the Oval sports ground. Pointing at it, she cries out, "Want ganstan!" She turns round to make sure that I've got the message. "My dad - ganstan!"

Playing amongst the grandstand's rows of benches has been a highlight of several previous visits to the park. We dump the pushchair at the base of one of the stand's stairways and climb up to the last row. I take a pew, open Lauren's bag of building blocks, and stretch out my legs. Far below us kids are criss-crossing the Oval's dry turf in a game of football.

Although I slept all morning, my body is still complaining at the beating I gave it last night. Ray and I did a gig for Sidney Lukakis at the Blue Note in Durban. A great little joint tucked away on an upper floor in Cuckoo Lane, the Blue Note has *the* crucial element as far as any jazzman is concerned - a core of regular patrons who dig bop. That ensures appreciation, good conversation, and an endless supply of free drinks and smokes. The vibe is rounded by the usual crowd thrown up by dockland - sailors, prostitutes, pimps, serious drinkers, druggies, and down-and-outers who've run into or lifted some dough. People on the edge, you know.

It was my last gig with Ray before he leaves for Joburg. We blew our sadness through its full range, starting in with mainly ballads and building up to almost a full set of up tempo hard bop. It was special stuff, by any standards. Afterwards we had a freaky encounter with two drunken sailors on our way out. We were passing them in the dimly lit stairwell when one grabbed Ray by the lapels of his raincoat.

"You think you're quite a guy, don't you nigger," he snarled.

I turned to intervene, but it was unnecessary. Ray kneed him viciously in the groin and as he doubled up punched him hard in the neck with his free hand.

"Run for it!" Ray shouted.

We hurtled down the steps and out onto the street. Without looking back we sprinted through the rain to the Morris Minor, both of us hugging our horns to our chests. When we reached it we leant against the heap on opposite sides, gasping for air in an empty street. Ray grinned across at me, and then we were both laughing helplessly.

The drive to Maritzburg passed quickly, although I took it slowly in the rain which just kept pissing down. We talked about Ray's big break. The leader of a successful big band in Sophiatown has given him a permanent blow, found him a place to stay, and got him a job in a city store. For most guys the decision to go would have been simple, but Ray is a sensitive cat with deep family and musical ties here.

We sat in silence for a long time after I pulled up outside his place. The sense of closeness, you know, was almost painful. Eventually he turned and looked at me.

"Phil, you will always stay here." He touched his chest. "You're the only white guy who has dug me as a man; not as a *black* man."

We shook hands and he got out. He put his fedora on before walking away.

I was feeling pretty cut up. Back home I took a bath, poured myself a brandy, and settled into a Raymond Chandler story. I hadn't finished it when Patty got up three hours later to start the day. I woke Lauren, dressed her for school, made us all breakfast, and saw them off before finishing the story with the last of the brandy. It must have been about nine when sleep at last overtook me.

My kip had hardly begun when the alarm clock split my head open in time to fetch Lauren. It's still wide open, suffering in all this sunshine.

Lauren abandoned the building blocks long ago to explore the terraced benches. Along then down, along then down, talking to herself all the time. When she reached the bottom row, she shouted up to me, demanding that I come and join her. I refused the summons, so she descended the stairs crab fashion and walked out onto the field. There she has made the acquaintance of a footballer sitting on the sidelines. They are kicking a ball to one another. I heave myself up and walk down to join them. He will lose patience with the game long before she will.

The footballer, a kid of about ten, smiles shyly as he passes the ball to me. For a few minutes we take turns delivering it to Lauren, who returns it with surprising skill. But quickly her weariness begins expressing itself in irritability, and I terminate the game. From her pushchair she waves her friend goodbye vigorously, and within yards of the Oval is fast asleep.

The transformation of our domestic scene is working well. Patty is a different person - you know, really *interested* in things she didn't care about after she stopped working. Like jazz, and the way she dresses. Tonight she's coming with me to a gig, the first time that's happened in Christ knows how long. I dig that. And other things, like my not having to get up every morning for the fucking workshop. And spending more time with Lauren. Bertha, of course, thinks the arrangement stinks:

"It's not good for a child not to have her mother at home. And the man of the house cooped up in a flat, imbuing his hobby while his wife sweats out a living in an office. Well!"

The fact that I earn more money indulging my hobby than Patty does from respectable employment makes no impression on her.

I stop for a breather at the top of the slope up to Grey's Hospital.

My life should be opening up, but frustrations with the Quintet are getting me down. Musically we're in a dead end street, but the other cats don't seem to see it. And there's a lot of resentment flying around because of all the other work I'm doing. I know it's justified - I mean it's pretty obvious that I have no commitment to the group anymore - but Jesus I have to stay *alive*.

Then I ask myself what this staying alive bit is all about. I mean, what am I really achieving? If I measure myself against the jazzmen who matter, the cats who have something to say and who contribute to music in saying it, then I'm a nobody. I kid myself that the Durban scene registers in the jazz world, but in the end it's also a dump. That's why Ray is leaving.

In the Chandler story I read last night, this gangster, you know, a really powerful guy, tells Marlowe that he's one of the world's nobodies, and that he will never be anything but a nobody. He was right, and Marlowe knew it. For Marlowe there is comfort in the fact that he doesn't give a damn. He possesses in abundance what the somebodies of this world seldom even understand - self-respect. I dig him tremendously for that - Jesus, he's a true hero if ever there was one. But I *do* give a damn.

At the bottom of the stairs leading up to the flat I lift Lauren out of the pushchair. She moans softly, but doesn't wake up. I fold up the chair and step into the entrance foyer. I pause at our postbox, then decide to leave Patty the pleasure of retrieving the post.

Inside I put Lauren down, pour myself a stiff drink, and stick a Dexter Gordon disc on the turntable. His horn, so different from Getz's, is sublime. It soothes my raw places although I cannot help thinking how unattainable it is. As I down the drink I tell myself that nevertheless, I have a contribution to make.

CHAPTER 20

Giving up pot has meant that I don't get to spend as much time in the yellow room. But my bowels, tired as ever, ensure that it remains familiar. I stretch back on the throne and return the gazes of the famous people spread out against the door. The mark of stardom - decorating the shithouses of nobodies.

The flat is silent. Patty has taken Lauren with her to the Brennans for the day. She wanted to get out of the flat, she said, but I know that the need to be away from me was greater.

I lift Bertrand Russell's *Problems* from my knees and take up where I left off on the last page. This must be my third reading of the bloody thing, and as always most of it makes good sense. I bring new insights to it this time round, in the interim having devoured a book by this bloody wonderful French cat Camus. Gladstone gave it to me with his highest commendation:

"Fucking dizzy stuff!" he said, with unGladstonian excitement.

It is. Some of the heavy analysis is beyond me, you know, but I dig his feeling for how we can make sense of life. In jazz terminology, the man swings.

So I hauled out this bible again to confirm its infallibility. Again and again it sounds the ring of truth, but somehow right at the heart of it, not always obvious, is a dull note which ruins the whole thing.

I finish the book, and bend forward to urge my bowels into action while I try to pinpoint the dull note. I think it's that Russell despises the personal view - from his lofty platform of the free intellect he has a panoramic view of universal knowledge. He can keep it. You carve out a personal significance or none at all.

In the last few days I've been doing a lot of carving. Not a very appropriate metaphor really, because control has lain someplace other than in my hands. Events started happening at the gig Patty came to. Run of the mill scene at the Thornville Hotel, you know, nothing out of the ordinary. Except for Patty that is. After the last set we sat around the band's table, enjoying one for the road before tackling the equipment. Then all hell broke loose. Gladstone set the charge and I pressed the plunger.

"Good news, guys," he said, blowing smoke out his nostrils.

He paused. The cat has a fine sense of the theatrical.

"I've got us a big one. That Durban outfit has pulled out of the dance at the Ants next Sunday. Guess who the manager wants to step in?"

The guys had been pretty pissed off at the Ansonia manager's original choice. We've done a lot of work there, and the dough is always good. Gladstone's news was greeted with a round of good-humoured banter.

I cut through the warm feelings: "I can't make it. I'm playing a gig in Durban next Sunday."

Trevor, our drummer, was the first to respond. "You'll have to cancel." He got up and walked over to the bandstand.

Bertie speared me with his eyes from the other side of the table. "Fuck me," he growled.

"Listen, I'm sorry," I said.

"Like fuck you are."

Patty had risen and was touching my shoulder. She wanted to get out.

Gladstone was sitting next to Bertie. He turned to him in an attempt to defuse things: "It's okay, dad. We'll make a plan."

"Fuck that! I'm tired of this tit gracing us with his presence when he feels like it. I'm tired of him running the show when he *is* around." He slammed his beer down. "And I'm tired of you always covering for him."

I got up to go.

"Hang on, Mister Cool," he said. "Gladstone, this is it. You choose him or me."

"Me too," Trevor said from the bandstand, where he was dismantling his drum kit.

"C'mon guys." Gladstone had been dragging heavily on his smoke. "Let's discuss this in a reasonable fashion."

"Fuck reasonable fashion. You have a choice. Make it a reasonable one."

I met Bertie's glare for a few moments, then spoke to Gladstone: "You have no obligation to me. I'm out, with no hard feelings."

Patty had grasped my hand. I turned and we walked out of the place.

I feel a delicate touch on the back of my head. I sit motionless and wait for Cat's next move. He is standing on the cistern, having come through the window above it. This is his favourite of three entrances to the flat. He licks my ear, then launches himself to the floor with a chirrup. His landing is messy for a cat, but he quickly regains his poise. Lazily he starts cleaning himself.

Patty and I did a lot of talking on the way back into town. I deflected her away from definite courses of action. Time to think was what I needed. I used up most of the next day thinking to little effect. Not that I was confused. A split had been on the cards for a long time, and I had a rough idea of what I wanted to do when it happened. The problem was Gladstone. God knows why, but I badly wanted him to make the split with me. Should I or shouldn't I try to nudge him into it?

Choppy waters. But as it turned out, the calm before another storm. With the post which Patty brought in that afternoon was another letter from Faith. I sat in the lounge, staring at the bulky envelope. My old work address had been scratched out and the flat's details scrawled alongside. Patty stood in front of me, waiting. She wasn't happy.

"For Chrissakes, honey. Yes, it is from Faith," I said.

Lauren was standing next to Patty, a fist clutching her dress. She pointed at the envelope. "See!"

Patty swept her up and disappeared into our bedroom.

I stared at the bloody thing for a long time before tearing it open. Ten pages of elegantly compact script. Jesus!

It was one of those rare letters which leave you feeling that you've been in a conversation. Faith had wanted to chat to me, and somehow she got her thoughts down with a directness which writing usually kills stone dead. Her big news was that she had completed her first recording date - two numbers on an album by a British big band I haven't heard of.

> "They're a good band, Phil, and successful. You would probably find them too old fashioned - stuck in the swing era - but they do swing. A far cry from most of the work I'm doing now. You wouldn't like it at all. Popular stuff with a jazzy feel to it, stinking of compromise, something I've become progressively better at."

She appears to be as happy as a bird, her only felt connections to this dump being a handful of relationships with people. Me being one of them. And, as she said three, four times, I don't belong here. London is the place to be; a place where jazzmen can make a mark even without compromising.

An important part of her happiness is a serious relationship she has with a guy called Victor. Serious enough for them to be planning a wedding early next year. Victor is a very wealthy medical doctor, specialising in one or other human orifice. He comes from a prominent English family, has worked in the States, and has homes in London and somewhere on the continent. The kind of guy who can help a chick forget about a mundane past. And someone with character, judging by the way he met Faith. She had gone to a party with another guy. Hash got passed around, and everyone ended up stoned. She woke up the next morning in Victor's house, still stoned and unable to remember meeting him the night before. He was also still stoned, and his formal greeting left Faith with the impression that he was claiming to be a vicar.

Not a word about the abortion. No reference to previous correspondence. Faith is one of those survivors who survive in style.

I found Patty in the kitchen. She stood stiffly before the stove.

"Honey, I want you to read it," I said from the doorway.

From the bathroom I could hear the sounds of Lauren's bath-time games.

I had given up hope of getting a response when Patty spoke in an empty, flat voice: "Please, let's not talk about it."

Cat is scratching at the door. I've stopped trying to persuade my bowels to behave like a normal organ, and am just sitting on the throne thinking. He looks at me, willing me to get up. I oblige him.

Patty retreated into an impenetrable silence which lasted almost a week. I tried to understand her; put myself in her place, you know, but ended up feeling resentful. After supper that night I ducked out for a walk and some company. I ended up at Johnny's place. He was lying on his bed, a joint in his hand, listening to a disc.

"How goes it?" he asked, lazily offering me the joint.

I shook my head and sat down on the bed. "Not so good."

We talked about the previous night. I wanted to know what had happened after Patty and I left.

"Plain zero. No one wanted to talk. We just packed up and split."
He stretched an arm out to his amp and dropped the volume. "So,
what are your plans?"

I outlined my idea of setting up a small outfit with James to work
the Indian town scene. I would rely on more work in Durban for real
dough, and in a year or so move down to Durban permanently - if
Patty would move, and if she could get a job there.

A long silence followed. The music stopped, and the only sound
in the room was the smacking of two moths against the light bulb.
Johnny was staring up at them, hands behind his head.

"How's this for a lekker plan?" he said. "Drop the Indian town
idea. Take me on, and we persuade Gladstone to come in too. With
James, that gives us a real classy quartet which could keep the
Quintet's work. Bertie and Trevor couldn't compete." He smiled.
"Master plan, hey?"

"You serious, dad?"

"Sure, baby. When you're tied up in Durban the rest of us would
make a neat Oscar Peterson trio. Or maybe we crack Durban
together."

I shook my head - disbelieving, you know. "Sounds great," I said.

He sat up. "Share a joint on it."

Again I refused. After some more natter I nipped over to the
mansion. Gladstone wasn't in, but I found him in the second pub I
dropped into. He was sitting at the Black Horse's bar, hunched over a
pint of ale. We talked until closing time, and on as we walked
through the quiet streets. He was pretty emotional, and when he
eventually agreed to Johnny's plan he kind of gave me a hug.

The next morning I sealed it at James' shop. That night we all got
together at Johnny's place, long discussion in the pot-sweet
atmosphere giving birth to what Johnny has dubbed The Glad Quartet.

Tonight we play our first gig. I check my watch as Cat nuzzles
my leg. Patty should be back any time now.

"Okay, dad, let's have something to eat," I say to Cat, and head
for the kitchen.

CHAPTER 21

The air was rarefied beneath a cloudless canopy whited out by the sun's reflections from a myriad dust particles. A relentless breeze cut through the town's streets from the snow-powdered peaks of the Drakensberg. It had swept away the dreams of spring nourished by a succession of warmer days. Wrapped in layers of material and wool, pedestrians turned inward to their bodies' sources of warmth as they hurried to their destinations. Philip was one of them, though his dress and relaxed demeanour set him apart. Pale face lifted to the breeze, hands thrust deep into the pockets of his dark brown sports jacket, he strolled down Church Street towards the Town Hall. The rest of his attire, including his dark glasses and a beret pulled low to one side of his head, were black. The beret was a gift from James du Bois to mark his feeling that the Glad Quartet should adopt an outward appearance suited to the hard bop character of their music. Only Gladstone had resisted - his sense of appropriate dress was impervious to such influences - the other three making dark glasses, berets, and casual, dark clothing standard attire for gigs.

Philip entered Market Square through the passage between the Town Hall and the public convenience. His dark, arrogant form was out of place in the modest proportions and mild hues of the dominantly Victorian townscape. It belonged beneath the sheer vertical lines of skyscrapers, on cosmopolitan streets possessed by vehicles and swarming humanity.

Philip was prizing out a memory vividly labelled by the colour white. He was a boy, one of a group from the Boys' Home herded onto a bus for an extraordinary adventure. For two days snow had fallen on the Natal midlands, leaving a thick carpet which reached the hills on the outskirts of town. The bus climbed Town Hill to the Hilton village, where the boys sprang out to experience delights they had only read about. Philip remembered withdrawing from the tangle. He had been unsettled by the alien environment into which they had been deposited. Familiar faces seemed unreal, subverted by shifting images from Charles Dickens, nursery rhymes and William stories.

He made his way through the reluctant activity of the market, hesitated at Twiggy's Pie Cart, and turned into Longmarket Street.

The Bombay Corner Hotel was just over a block away on the edge of Indian town. The last time Philip had seen Fat was nearly a month before, when he and Patty had been honoured guests at Daddy's funeral. The occasion had been an exotic combination of Christian, Hindu and New Orleans traditions. The burial at the Mountain Rise cemetery followed a crowded but restrained Anglican service. Emotion was released at the graveside, where Philip was part of a band which played blues numbers before the ceremony and raucous New Orleans marches after Daddy had been laid to rest. Back at the New Scotland Road house, Fat laid on a lavish reception in a marquee which all but filled the garden. Philip, pressed into it by Fat and Patty, delivered one of many commemorative speeches. A garland of flowers around his neck, his voice soft and deliberate, he spoke briefly of his respect for a man who had shared in the immemorial feeling of jazz.

At the Hotel reception Philip was told that Fat was busy with a client but would not be long. He sat down on a deep chair covered in a material richly patterned in shades of red. It was part of a suite, set off by a bright turquoise carpet, which matched the luxurious curtains hung across the full length of one wall. The kind of décor which a visitor to the Taj Mahal might expect to find. A commonplace note was sounded by the black and white photographs of jazzmen which hung on the wall behind him and the blackboard at the entrance on which a forthcoming gig was advertised in multi-coloured chalk. Since taking over sole ownership, Fat had made his mark.

A door opened and Fat emerged with his visitor. He saw him out before noticing Philip as he turned back to his office. His face lit up.

"Ah, Phil, what a pleasure!" He shook Philip's hand with both of his. "Come in and have a drink."

Fat had put on weight. His jowls trembled against an immaculate collar. Despite the cold, perspiration beaded the unhealthy pallor of his brow. Having ordered a brandy for Philip, he ushered him into a room which was startlingly plain in comparison with the reception area.

"So, dad, where've you been? You avoiding me?" Philip asked, referring to a couple of calls which Fat had not returned.

Fat squeezed himself into his chair and mopped his brow with an expansive handkerchief.

"Not at all, Phil," he said, folding the handkerchief neatly into a square. "I have been very busy - business, always business, family, the church - you know how it goes."

Philip's drink arrived. Fat poured himself a glass of water from a jug and they clinked glasses.

"Tell me, Phil, how is your new band faring?" He pointed at Philip's beret. "I see James is making an impact."

"It's not my group. We have no leader - it's more of a collective scene, you know. We're doing well; nothing spectacular, but we have enough work to make us viable."

Fat smiled. "No doubt it is fair to assume that the *sound* is spectacular."

"Like wow," Philip said, face raised to the ceiling, eyes closed. He dug a forefinger into his beret. "This carries a message - integrity before viability."

They smiled at each other.

"I'm glad, Phil."

"But seriously, dad, no kidding, this quartet is something else. The standard we're maintaining is exceptional, and we're extending ourselves - musically, you know - all the time." He gulped down a mouthful of brandy. "It's the most meaningful work I've ever done."

"You must excuse my apparent lack of interest recently. Things have been..." Fat swung both hands from side to side in front of him. He was sunk low in his chair. "I would very much like to engage the Quartet some time soon."

"That would be cool, dad. But tell me about things." Philip imitated Fat's hand movements.

A faint smile hovered about Fat's mouth and was gone. He dropped his head back and stared at the ceiling. His hands wrestled one another fiercely on the table. "It is a sad time in my life. First my father, now my home." He continued after a long pause, his gaze still directed upward. "Friends in the Liberal Party have informed me that it is only a matter of time before the Group Areas Act is enforced here. I've decided to sell up while I can still get a good price, and move out to Raisethorpe. My brother, the one in Pentrich, is doing the same."

"Jeeze, dad, I'm sorry." A hand strayed to his packet of cigarettes, then dropped.

Fat lowered his gaze to meet Philip's. "I have been afraid of this for a long time. It was really inevitable. And yet ... and yet the hurt is so deep." Tears slid from his eyes down his round cheeks.

Spontaneously Philip reached across and placed a hand on Fat's.

***

Philip felt more empty than angry. His aversion for things political left him without the means to focus anger. He knew only that the whole fabric of society stank.

The breeze had stiffened; it tugged at his clothing as he walked back up Longmarket Street. He passed the market, the statue of Queen Victoria beneficent before the colonial legislative buildings, and turned into Theatre Lane, one of the numerous pedestrian lanes which dissect the town centre's long blocks.

He was almost upon her before he noticed Faith's mother. She was standing outside her shop at the entrance to an arcade, appraising a new window display. He tucked in his chin and quickened his pace.

"Mr Maddison?" she enquired as he passed her.

Oh Christ, he thought, slowing down and walking backwards away from her.

"Yes, hello Mrs Woolmer," he called. "Sorry I can't chat; I have an appointment."

With an artificial smile he turned and fled. Round the corner in Church Street he stopped to light himself a cigarette. He stood in the shelter of a shop entranceway, drawing in the soothing flavour of the Texan while he decided that bumping into people you would prefer not to see was a characteristic of a dump.

It was late morning when he turned into the driveway of Johnny's place. Johnny's mother, a large woman with ravaged visage but warm nature, was sweeping the verandah.

"Johnny in?" Philip asked.

"When is he not?" she countered. "Ja, skattie, he's in his room."

Johnny was out of work. More precisely, he was between jobs, a perennial state for him. Most of his jobs were in the railways, secured by his father, who had worked as a train driver all his adult life. Johnny simply could not face doing all day what others told him to do. He would stick at it out of a sense of duty to his parents until he was too depressed to get out of bed in the morning; enjoy a period of freedom and psychological rehabilitation; then, when the sense of duty reasserted itself, start looking for another job.

Philip rapped on his door and stepped inside, into a dense warmth emanating from two heaters placed strategically at opposite ends of the room. Johnny lay on his back, feet embedded in his pillow, dead to the noises of Philip's entrance. His open mouth was pink in the dark stubble of his unshaven cheeks; a hand grasped a tangle of greasy hair. Philip closed the door and wandered over to Johnny's record collection. It was laid out in neat piles across one side of the room. With difficulty he extracted one and placed it on the turntable. As the crackles died he stepped to the bed and watched Johnny. The urgent notes of Herb Ellis' guitar filled the room.

Johnny grunted, shifted position, opened one eye. He grinned.

"Jesus, Phil, I was dreaming this chick was doing wonderful things for me. What a disappointment."

Philip feigned a blow to his stomach, then sat down on the bed.

"So, what's doing, main dad?" Johnny said. The appellation, applied since the formation of the Quartet, was tacit recognition of Philip's leadership.

"Feeling bum, you know - in need of edification."

"Well, baby, you've come to the right place."

Philip told him about Fat. While he talked Johnny rolled a joint and lit up. They passed it back and forth. It was the first joint he had smoked since his promise to Patty.

"I don't know," Philip concluded. "The powerful are so fucking powerful in this country."

"It's the same everywhere," Johnny said.

Philip shook his head, in resignation rather than disagreement. "Sure, in a way that's true. But it's so fucking obscene here." He pulled at his goatee. "You know, before she left, Faith argued with me about Joburg. She said it and the whole bloody country is a dump. I reckon she was right."

Johnny was sitting with his back against the wall. He pulled his knees up to his chest. They listened to the music, both caught up in their own thoughts. When the number was through, Johnny spoke:

"You know, Phil, if it wasn't for jazz, life itself would be a dump."

CHAPTER 22

The butterfly's wings had opened again. It took Patty more than a week to quell the demons set loose by Faith's second letter. Released, reluctantly at first, by Philip, she retreated into a private world to do battle with them. When she emerged, weary, vulnerable, Philip's wordless resumption of closeness was a balm. Moved by the depth of her hurt, and revitalised by the formation of the Quartet, Philip was better equipped than at any other time to accommodate the complex energies of their relationship. Instinctively he shied an intellectual processing of what had happened. So the wings of their love, drawing on mutual relief and gladness, spread a broader, subtly differentiated range of colour.

This heralded an interlude which both of them would remember as idyllic. Philip's surge of creativity was reinforced by her renewed interest in his music. Every other week she drew a party of friends together to attend one of the Quartet's gigs. This placed firmly behind them another aspect of the deviation in their course fashioned by Lauren's advent. An almost unnoticed backdrop to the interlude, but an element which was to lodge in both their memories, was the advance of spring, with its longer afternoons and warm evenings.

The interlude closed with what turned out for them to be the momentous visit to South Africa of the American bandleader Bobby Ryder. Ryder was a prominent figure in the burgeoning West Coast jazz industry, a prolific recording artist noted for his ability to attract outstanding musicians into his medium-size combinations. He was no innovator. A product of the New York jazz scene, he applied in Los Angeles and San Francisco a recipe introduced successfully by others - careful arrangement of an essentially bop sound, the exclusion of excesses attendant on introverted individuals being allowed too much scope, and a final product accessible to a wide audience. He was brought to South Africa on a lightning tour, playing two gigs in Johannesburg and three in Durban with local musicians. His wife, the jazz singer Sue Connors, accompanied him.

His dates in Durban were all at the Shah Jehan, a capacious venue attracting racially diverse audiences. The Glad Quartet and partners piled into two cars to attend the first one. Ryder, a competent but unexciting alto saxophonist, played through the formal gig with a Durban combination. Connors sang the middle sets, mainly Gershwin and Berlin numbers. She was a very swinging singer, blessed with a delightfully sure feel for the blues, but she drank heavily that night, began to lose her way, and eventually disappeared from the stand.

Afterwards Ryder jammed into the small hours with whoever wanted to play. Philip joined him with the Sydney Lukakis band, immediately establishing a rapport with him. As Philip told Patty afterwards, "This cat has an incredible feel for where I'm going, you know; he's all about respect and support. A wonderful facilitator." During a break, as the Quartet's partners were prizing them loose for the journey home, Ryder took Philip aside and invited him to play the next gig. He brushed aside Philip's expressions of doubt: "I'll arrange things. No sweat."

True to his word, he phoned the next day to confirm the arrangement. With Gladstone Philip made the date in standard Gladstonian mode - very late start, high speed travel in the Ford, moderately late arrival. Johnny and James had decided to give it a miss, neither being particularly impressed by Ryder. The gig followed a similar pattern to the first one, although Sue Connors was conspicuous by her absence.

After a short jam session, Ryder invited Philip and Gladstone to share a drink with him in his hotel room. The drink turned into half a dozen as the three men talked jazz. Ryder was articulate, interested in the South African jazz scene, and interesting on the latest developments in the United States. Twice their conversation was interrupted by Connors shuffling through the small lounge area on her way to the bathroom. A sock tied around her head, eyes barely open, she gave no indication of having noticed them. Both times Ryder, without discernible embarrassment, excused himself in order to assist her. He was, in Philip's terms, a cool guy.

After about the fourth drink he disclosed the purpose of his invitation. He had just lost his tenorman and Philip was *the* man for the job. The band's next major engagement started in six weeks. He wanted Philip in Los Angeles at least a week before then.

Philip took a while to absorb Ryder's words. The brandies had dulled his head. He threw out the obvious objections - Patty and Lauren, the Quartet, no money to get to Los Angeles, no passport.

The black cats raised a lot of dust over the cultural boycott. They wouldn't bite unless he could secure approval for the visit from local political and cultural organisations. No problem, he assured us. But months of uncertainty followed. At first the Interim Cultural Desk in Johannesburg approved in principle, but decreed that it should be linked to a concert for returning exiles which was being planned. Then they demanded that they should participate in organising the visit. The club owner accepted that, but negotiations fell apart when the Desk split into competing factions. At the same time it became obvious that the big concert would never take place.

By that stage I was pissed off by the whole scene. The makers of cultural rules and regulations in South Africa seem to operate in the same way as the functionaries who fucked up the country in the fifties. They threaten everything that jazz stands for. I thought I was long past making statements, but here was the time to make one. The club owner's original invitation had picked up enough credibility in the messy exercise to make it viable, so three of us decided to accept it. I cleared space in my schedule - a week to look up friends and visit Lauren, followed by two weeks playing gigs and doing workshops in Johannesburg.

"Are you excited?" Patty asks, screwing up her eyes against the afternoon sun. The illumination probes harshly the imprints of age in her face.

"I'm too old for that," I reply.

She shakes her head, a smile playing about her mouth.

A long silence follows until we enter the outskirts of the village where she lives with her happy family. A clean, neat place designed for happy homes.

"Would you like to read Lauren's letter?" she asks.

"Sure."

"It's such a happy letter. She and Ed are so looking forward to your visit."

We turn into the driveway which leads to the large, rambling house. She stops the car next to the front door with a jerk, then turns to me.

"Well, here we are. Phil, aren't the changes in South Africa wonderful? It'll be great for you to see them at first hand." She opens her door. "And, for the first time in how many years we can stop worrying about Lauren and Ed getting into trouble."

After I've unpacked we share a pot of tea in the sitting room. David is giving art classes in Bath and the boys are playing cricket. I ask after them, then listen politely as Patty relates their many achievements since I was last here. I'm desperate for a smoke, but smoking inside is not allowed.

"But enough about us. How goes it in the new house?"

I have recently uprooted myself from my bungalow in Stoke Poges and moved into a run-down semi-detached in Bloomsbury. It was a long time coming - years of isolation from friends in the city, the grind of maintaining a big property, and the exhausting car, train and tube journeys in for gigs made the move attractive. But searching property columns and braving estate agents was always just beyond me. Then Faith found this bargain in Bloomsbury and got the wheels turning. Even got me mildly enthusiastic about renovating the place. But the rotations exhausted the shit out of me, and I find myself in a chaos I'm too weary to even think about attacking.

"Fucking awful, really," I say, fingering the pack of Texans in my jacket pocket.

CHAPTER 24

The small plane bounces an air pocket in a sky busy with cloud formations. It is early evening, multiple shafts of light slashing the plane's heaven into shades of white, pale blue and pink. The pilot has just announced that bad weather over Pietermaritzburg might force a diversion to Durban. His voice was barely audible above the high pitched roar of the motors, which holds the half empty cabin in a relentless grip. Philip did not hear it. His attention is focused on keeping his book, a large coffee table volume, reasonably steady. He curses as the plane pitches wildly, throwing him against the fuselage. Beer spills onto the book from the can held firmly against his knee. For some while he occupies himself absorbing the beer into the cuff of one of his shirtsleeves.

The book is one of Terence Conran's handsome productions on interior design. Bought in the wavelet of enthusiasm which coincided with his move from Stoke Poges to Bloomsbury, it was quickly abandoned. Now, right away from the debilitating influence of the mess in his home, he has determined to formulate an offensive strategy using the book he came upon while packing.

The lurching of the plane has made reading impossible. He removes his reading glasses and with his body probes the chair for a more comfortable position. Before finding it, he leans forward to check his saxophone on the empty seat in front of him. Satisfied, he turns to the porthole as he takes a swig of beer. Clouds have all but enveloped the plane in swathes of grey and dark purple. A small light flashes bravely from a wing tip, appearing to accompany rather than be part of the plane. Philip watches it, his greying hair pressed against the window's inside layer of plastic. He is wondering how Denis, his feline companion of several years, is faring alone in the house. Denis is a neutered female, named after Margaret Thatcher's husband for its unfeline stupidity and devotion. Deciding to leave Denis in the care of a friend who lives nearby so soon after the trauma of the move from Stoke Poges was probably the hardest part of accepting the invitation to play in South Africa.

***

"I've heard so much about you, Philip. Gladstone thinks the sun shines out of you." The woman's round face breaks into a throaty laugh.

"Oh shut up, sausage," Gladstone says, handing her a sherry.

Another laugh fades into a smoker's wheeze. Her eyes shine merrily, attesting more readily than any other part of her to a beauty that has faded. When she married Gladstone fifteen years ago it was in its final bloom.

Jesus, he's an old man, Philip thinks as he watches Gladstone shuffling back to the drinks' cabinet. Denise's motherly care cannot stem the attrition of ulcers and a failing heart.

"Still into brandy, Phil?" Gladstone's voice is tired, like the eyes in his wasted face.

"Sure, dad. Make it a double."

Philip looks around him as Gladstone potters interminably before the cabinet. Park View's sitting room is dominated by a television set, around which a modern lounge suite is grouped. He looks for but cannot see any hi-fi equipment. Together with Gladstone's record collection, it was taken in a burglary years ago, and has not been replaced. Philip can recognise nothing but the contours of the room's shell.

Denise is telling him about the Collins Five, Gladstone's latest band, which is keeping him busy and bringing in a nice amount of pocket money. She has taken out her knitting, the clicking of the needles providing an up tempo rhythm for her voice.

"Mind if I smoke?" Philip interrupts her.

"Of course not, dear." She giggles. "As long as you don't try to get Gladstone to join you. We've both given up."

Philip is lighting up when Gladstone puts his drink and an ashtray on a table next to him. For a moment he stands still, slightly stooped and seemingly uncertain, fingering his watch. Philip gazes at him through the cloud of smoke he has expelled. He wonders if he hasn't perhaps taken Gladstone's favourite chair. The interference of loose ends accumulated during the more than thirty years in which they have had no contact is tangible.

"Phil, would you mind if we watched the news just now?" Gladstone asks. "These days you never know what FW and Mandela might have up their sleeves."

"Do sit down, pet," Denise says. "Philip doesn't want to feel that he is in a station, now does he?"

Gladstone shuffles to an empty chair as Denise asks Philip what he thinks of the New South Africa:

"I would love to know how it looks from a British perspective."

Philip grunts. "I was never good at big questions. Let's just say that it's encouraging."

She sips her sherry as she formulates another question.

"You comfortable, dad?" Gladstone asks.

Philip nods, then, to sidestep Denise, says to him, "So, you've been in the mansion all these years?"

"No. I've been around, you know. Came back to look after Mother when Father died."

"And no thanks to Peter Collins that we're here today," Denise says. "You knew Peter, didn't you?" She leans towards Philip eagerly.

"Please, sausage," Gladstone interjects, "Phil doesn't want to hear family gossip."

"He did his damnedest to stop Gladstone getting this house," she sails on. "Excuse my French, but he's a typical little shit of a lawyer."

Philip leans forward to stab out his cigarette, barely disguising a leer.

"Hardly," Gladstone protests. "He hasn't practised for years."

"Is he still into politics?" Philip cuts across a retort from Denise.

"Who knows," Gladstone replies. "Chasing the big buck became more important to him in the sixties. He left the firm behind and got involved in all kinds of business operations. I've kind of lost track, you know." He grins. "Our paths don't cross."

"Of course he's still into politics." Denise holds out her empty glass towards Gladstone. "Not the kind he used to be into. But everyone knows he's hand in glove with the KwaZulu government." She shakes her glass impatiently.

"So he's dropped the separatist bit, huh?"

"Not really," Denise replies, leaning towards Philip. "They want a separate Natal-KwaZulu in a sort of federal system."

"Who's they?"

"Well, KwaZulu ..." Denise flutters her free hand dramatically. "And a lot of people in Natal."

Philip nods, then mumbles to himself rather than to the others, "At least blacks are included in the deal."

A triumphant smile spreads Denise's face. "The 'New South Africa', Philip. Now..."

"And the separatist scene as a whole," Philip interrupts. "Gone the same way?"

Gladstone has shuffled across the room to retrieve Denise's glass. He stares into it as he responds. "The arseholes scattered far and wide. Their fear of Afrikaners was overtaken by their fear of blacks."

A silence follows his statement. Before Denise can break it, Philip changes tack.

"That chick Peter was married to? They still together?"

Denise snorts. "He's *into* number three now dear."

After the news and supper Denise hovers briefly, putting things away, checking that the doors are locked. She excuses herself after reminding Gladstone to take his medicines and warning him not to have more than one drink.

"Philip, please don't let him keep you up all night. He doesn't get tired until the early hours, then sleeps through to lunch time." She pauses to kiss Gladstone on the crown of his head. "Nightie, pet."

Alone, they talk about the jazz world. Gladstone is keen to hear of Philip's experiences with the big names. After a few drinks they both begin to relax. Gladstone accepts a Texan, confiding that he still smokes the odd cigarette when Denise is at work. He coughs after his first puff.

"These are fucking bombs - I stick to ultra milds these days." He grins. "Jesus, dad, you're looking great. I expected a wreck to get off that plane."

The grin draws a fleeting hint of the youthful Gladstone across his face. Philip notices it, and feels the sadness which has inhabited him all evening penetrate deeper.

"So tell me about the Glad Quartet," he says. "You cats achieve great things or what?"

Until now he has sidestepped references to their shared past. He is reluctant to release a discussion which inevitably will disturb the lines memory has drawn.

"That was a great band, Phil. We hung around here for a while after you left, then moved down to Durban. We really cracked it for... I don't know, maybe a year. Until Johnny committed suicide."

"What?"

"A tragic scene, that. You remember how he was always into dope, even as a kid? In Durban he suddenly chucked it, got himself a steady girlfriend, quite a classy chick, really seemed to be settling down. But there must have been something raging inside him. I don't know, maybe there were hassles with the chick. One night after a gig he drove his bike flat out straight into a wall. Someone saw him do it."

"Christ," Philip murmurs. He finds it impossible to place the story behind an interval of three decades.

"After that, Du Bois and I went our separate ways. I played with Sidney Lukakis - remember him? - for a while, but most of the time worked on my own. You know the 'background music for elegant diners' scene. When Father died I came back here."

For a long time they sit in a silence broken only by the ticking of a clock on the mantelpiece.

"What about Fat Singh? You see much of him?"

"He was always around, you know. But he died way back, in the sixties. Heart attack."

***

Soon after midnight Philip pleaded weariness and climbed up the familiar stairs to the guest room. A bath served only to reinforce his heaviness. He stands at the bedroom window, naked, smoking his third cigarette in a row. His body is lean with a hardness that removes it a generation from Gladstone's decaying form.

The only movement outside is that of an occasional car sliding past in surreal metallic passage through a suffusion of orange light. Philip's thoughts stray back to the plane's landing earlier in the evening. Without warning it broke through a bank of clouds lying low over the city. Right beneath them a myriad lights spread in all directions, lines of orange marking the bigger roads. As the plane descended Philip discerned the shapes of buildings, the dark patches of open spaces. But he found no point of orientation; recognised nothing.

He leans out the open window to flick his butt into the garden. Pushing a hand through his hair, he sighs. It was a mistake to come back, he tells himself.

CHAPTER 25

I suppose the trees must be taller, and the paint on the pavilion roof less than thirty years old. But as I look out over the Alexandra Park oval from the back row of benches, what I see slides neatly into the place shaped for it by my memory. Although the ground is deserted, I can transpose the footballers of those winter afternoons in 1955 without strain. All morning I have been seeking just such a correlation between present and past; now that my need has been satisfied, I am left feeling unsettled.

Doing the musical rounds in England I must have seen scores of village greens. Through jaundiced eyes, granted - the bright green of foliage is still my least favourite colour. The oval below me is as picturesque as the best of them. Not that I am a connoisseur of the outdoors, you know, but the years I spent in Stoke Poges kind of eroded my predisposition for artificially illuminated cityscapes. Well, maybe the process was nothing more than a guy getting old and finding things like cleanliness and quietness more attractive. My favourite haunt around Stoke Poges was the Burnam Birches, an incredibly dense wood with towering trees and grassless floor. I dig its closeness, and the fact that in most parts the sun barely penetrates the forest cover. Its lines are all vertical, reaching up like the pillars of a vast natural cathedral. If anything can stir in me even a hint of religious sensibility it's the Birches.

My morning kicked off in the mansion's kitchen with Denise and a full English breakfast. She bustled around me in a bright pink dressing gown, her long hair untied and wild, seeming to take pleasure in every mouthful I forced into my chops. Usually the combination of wild activity and committed eating that early in the morning would have been deadly. But after last night it was kind of soothing. I had been jerked from one dream to the next, almost surfacing repeatedly, but never sufficiently to get up and clear my head. Until the last one that is, the one that woke me just before dawn. I remember it clearly. A motorbike, one of those monsters, with me steering and Patty clutching on from behind. We turned a corner and raced straight towards a brick wall. The bricks were misshapen, hostile. I wanted to smash them. Patty screamed as I accelerated into the wall. I started waking as we went through it without any resistance, and broke into consciousness with an image of Gladstone sitting at a sidewalk café on the other side of the wall smiling serenely at us.

After breakfast I ducked out for a walk. I spent a while up near the railway station searching for Johnny's place. A way of paying last respects? I don't know. Then I ambled down Church Street to the Town Hall. The street has been transformed into one unholy balls up. Partly pedestrianised, it is decorated with pseudo Victorian bits and pieces, most of the shops have been fronted by characterless facades, and the traffic is channelled by a row of penis-like columns. The Town Hall, newly restored by the looks of it, was a welcome relief. Beyond it I found the market gone, replaced by a car park and a naked hunk of a building. Where the public shithouse was, is a fountain with modest jets of water which reminded me of nothing so much as the arcs of piss heavily laden drinkers produce. An inspired creation. Feeling better, I took off down Commercial Road, past the cemetery, and into the park.

***

We stand on the pavement's edge, leaning against the bright yellow Jaguar that is Gladstone's joy. Before us, surrounded by suburban bungalows, is the Italian prisoner of war church. It looks smaller than I remember it. Above the front door in bold script are the words:

MATRI
DIVINAE GRATIAE
CAPTIVI ITALICI
A.D. MCMXLIV

A simple inscription on an unused building, but powerful to move me. Christ. Are there any joys without the undertow of pain?

"Take a closer decko?" Gladstone asks.

"Nah."

I prefer to look at it from a distance, as we did from the perimeter fence of the camp when we were kids.

Traffic drones on a nearby highway as I allow my memories to run. Gladstone is getting restless when at last I speak.

"When we went to Italy on holiday I made a point of looking up Peschiera. It was just as Roberto described it."

"Jesus. Roberto." He weighs the memory, turns it about. "And?"

"We only stayed for a day. Did a coach trip from there right around Lake Garda. I had planned to try and find Roberto, but when we got there, I don't know, it seemed like a stupid thing to do. Perhaps if I had been alone it would have been different. But being with Patty and Lauren somehow placed him irrevocably in the past."

I'm not being on the level. Patty and Lauren may have been a factor, but deep down I know that I just didn't want to risk spoiling one of my only happy childhood memories.

"When was that?"

"Jesus, I don't know. Somewhere in the mid-sixties, soon after we left the States."

He glances at me, and I know that he wants to ask me about Patty. But he's a sensitive cat, you know.

"That's something I never understood, Phil. Your leaving the States I mean. You were playing with some great musicians, doing a lot of recording. After you left you dipped out of sight. I picked up the odd reference to you in the magazines, but London was right out of the mainstream." He prods at his mouth with a thumb. "Relatively speaking."

I ponder the implied question, attempting to dredge up the long-buried complex of factors.

"American society must be the most stimulating on earth," I say. "The buzz is urgent, you know, people aren't afraid to give their dreams their best shot. And resources are available to even the most way out dreamers. But there's another side. Christ, dad, you've read Chandler, Bud Schulberg, those cats. The parading of Americanism and obeisance to the dollar on television, in Hollywood, in Congress, *everywhere*. And always in terms of a moral superiority which makes the powerful in this country appear naive." I pause, conscious that I am sermonising. "For a while, marginally, you know, I got into the Beat scene."

I hope the conversation will move into a discussion of Allen Ginsberg, Jack Kerouac and the other apostles of the alternative society. But Gladstone isn't biting.

"So that's why you left?" he asks innocently.

"No. It was the context. I got a good offer from London at a time when there were a lot of hassles in the Ryder band. And Patty wasn't happy in LA, you know, wouldn't have been happy anywhere in the States."

"Ah," he says, nodding. "Did Patty ever tell you that she visited me once when she was out to see her folks?"

"Yeah. Yeah she did."

He is staring at the church. "A lovely person. One of the best."

I rack my brains for a way of heading him off without hurting his feelings.

"You know Phil, until I met Denise Patty was the only woman I had ever been able to really relax with. She had - how can I put it? - a kind of serene aura."

"She hasn't changed."

He turns to me. "You still see her?"

"Yeah. We're good friends."

I can almost hear his mind ticking over trying to select the next question.

"So ..." I pause to sniff. "You were going to tell me about the Ansonia gigs."

"Yes." He nods meditatively. "Yes. I hope you don't mind about tonight?"

Gladstone has arranged a gig at the Ansonia Hotel to coincide with my visit. He's advertised it with me as the star attraction, and invited Durban notables to come and share in the privilege. And, the cherry on top, has set up an interview with a reporter from the local paper. Jesus Christ!

I take in the vulnerable look on his dial. "Nah," I say. "Glad to oblige."

**

It must be about two in the morning. I lie on my back, checking out the mound in the blanket where my feet are. It is silhouetted against the faint orange of the window, and, like the rest of me, is motionless. I breathe as shallowly as possible, my shoulders propped up against two pillows. The pain in my chest burns up towards my throat with each inhalation. I tell myself for the umpteenth time that at least it is not on my left side, so it can't be my fucking heart packing in. When it first appeared, a few months back after a gig in London, I dismissed it as bad heartburn. This is maybe its sixth reappearance, always when I've been blowing, and I know that it can't be heartburn. An unpleasant image of Denise bringing in morning tea to a stiff lodges in my brain, gathering to it thoughts like the appropriateness of my dying here tonight - you know, small town boy who has made it overseas returns to keel over after one final blow.

The blow wasn't one I would want to be remembered by. The other guys were pretty revved up, and the sound wasn't bad, but I missed my groove altogether. I started on the wrong foot from the moment Gladstone swung the Jaguar into the Ansonia's grounds. What I saw made me angry. The long, sloping lawn with tables under rows of palm trees has been replaced by a tarred car park. Great memories - afternoons with friends under the palms, enjoying quiet drinks, sometimes with hot frankfurters and mustard, watching kids playing between the tables - were alienated, irrationally perhaps, by a stretch of tar and the few remaining palms with the bottom of their trunks obscenely covered in white paint. The press interview did nothing to improve my mood. The reporter was a young babe who knew nothing about music, let alone jazz. She pushed the human interest and political angles, and expended a lot of energy trying to get my views on the cultural boycott.

"When did you go into exile, Mr Maddox?" she asked.

I took my time over that one. "I've never been an exile. If you must have a label, I think 'vagrant' would be more appropriate."

The pain is beginning to ease. I lever myself higher up against the pillows and retrieve my half empty glass of brandy. A few sips down the hatch and I begin to feel human again.

The gig did have its moments. Sidney Lukakis is still playing a swinging horn. Gladstone shed years as he built up a sweat directing operations and pumping the rhythm section. And it was great to see James du Bois again. He didn't play - hasn't played in years - but the cat still has jazz in his bones.

"Philip, this," he gestured around him, "is the exception. Gladstone plays here once a month, for peanuts baby. For the rest, the dudes in management demand a menu of slightly jazzed up pop. And the scene is exactly the same in Durban. When bop lost currency, I sold my bass and took up stamp collecting."

We laughed.

"But no kidding, Phil, what we had was special. Compromising it would have been a kind of death. To quote you, 'integrity before viability'."

I get up slowly, nervous of disturbing the pain's steady retreat. Footsteps shuffle along the corridor outside my room - Gladstone has found the weariness he waits for before attempting to kip, and is on his way to join Denise. I move across to the window.

James has got his life together. He put down his horn without bitterness and ploughed his energies into making his business successful. I've come a long way to meet my first really hip businessman.

CHAPTER 26

Philip is sprawled in a low armchair, brandy in hand.

"Jeeze Lol, I dig your place the most."

"To say the least?" Lauren replies with a mischievous grin.

She is sitting opposite him in a chair of similar shape but different covering. Her bare legs are folded under her, and she holds a tall glass of beer in both hands. She wears a khaki T-shirt, its inscription 'Free the children!' obscured by her glass. The chairs are part of a cluster about a karakul rug at one end of an open space occupying almost the whole of the house's upper floor. The space is broken in the centre by a broad stairway leading up from ground level around which grouped pieces of furniture provide casually delineated smaller areas. Paintings and posters cover the white walls in a busy counterpoint to the stretches of empty wooden floor.

"Just one discordant note."

She inclines her head, a tress of her straight, blonde hair falling across her face.

"The music, honeybee."

A Bob Dylan compact disc is playing, one of a collection of mainly rock music from the late sixties and seventies. This is a more recent recording, Dylan's rough but nasal voice intoning divine disapproval of materialism.

"Sorry, Phil - I had forgotten how bloody old-fashioned you are. Shall I take it off?"

"Nah. Just kidding."

Divergence in musical taste has been a constant in their relationship. Lauren's musical sensibility was shaped by her adolescent experience of London in the sixties, the defining influence, as for so many of her generation, being the later sound of the Beatles. Jazz she can relate to only in the context of live performance.

"Excuse me, buggers."

The top half of a male torso extrudes from the stairway. Ed has been trying to attract their attention.

"Ah, the voice of the turtle," Lauren responds.

Ed laughs. "No, lover, the voice of the fucking cook. Phil, how do you like your curry?"

Cooking is one of Ed's hobbies. Throughout the fourteen years he and Lauren have been together, the kitchen has been his domain. Peaceful accomplishment there provides an ideal antidote to the sustained pressure of his work as a human rights lawyer.

A long, relaxed silence follows his departure. When Lauren rises to attend to the compact disc player, Philip also gets up. He examines the wall behind his chair, stopping before a large reproduction of the ANC logo.

"What's the ballpoint scrawl?" he asks without turning.

Lauren joins him. She puts an arm round his waist. "That is Oliver Tambo's signature. He did it for me when I was in Lusaka last year. I was part of a delegation of whites from inside the country which was invited to meet with the ANC."

He nods. "So you support the ANC?"

"With qualification, yes."

He looks down at the face which reminds him of Patty. It has the same plainness around the large Brennan blue eyes, but unlike Patty's is burnt brown by the sun. An open face, untouched by make-up. He bends to kiss her forehead.

"And all the violence - do you think it can be sorted out?"

She shrugs. "It's easy to despair, Phil. But we *must* sort it out."

She works for a rural development agency which has built its reputation on fighting the forced removal of communities. Peripherally involved in anti-apartheid activities from her return to South Africa in 1976, she gave up her academic career soon after the first state of emergency in the eighties to pursue them full time. Politics is the warp and woof of the life she shares with Ed, her commitment inevitably drawing her into frequent confrontation with the state. She has been arrested a number of times, and on one occasion spent two days in a police station cell. Her infrequent letters to Philip have contained only vague allusions to these activities.

"Tell me about your work," Philip says.

After supper, eaten from their laps in the lounge area, Ed entertains Phil with accounts of his sometimes bizarre experiences with the police. That morning he spoke to a senior security policeman who claimed to be looking forward to the assumption of power by the ANC, on the grounds that he would have just as much work to do and be better paid for it. Ed has almost daily contact with the police, and has been forced to build relationships informed by more than unbridled hostility.

"There've been some surprising rewards. I suppose they apply in any professional relationship, but I've found patience and a sense of humour indispensable. Of course there are the real bastards, a lot of them, with whom nothing works."

"They're all bastards," Lauren says. She is sitting on the rug, her back against Ed's legs.

"Perhaps it's a question of semantics, but I know there are some ordinary people squeezed into those uniforms," he responds.

Philip has met Ed on only two previous occasions, at the wedding and during a fleeting visit to London five years ago, but he knows that he likes him.

As they descend the stairs at the end of the evening, Ed turns to him: "Phil, why don't you stay with us the whole time you're here? Your friend is also welcome."

Philip has booked into a hotel with Faith. He is defensive about their relationship, and has always avoided the subject with Lauren.

"I appreciate that, Ed," he says. "Thanks, but ..."

"But no thanks," Lauren completes his sentence, smiling at him mischievously.

***

Lauren's friendship with Philip was formed during a university vacation she spent with him in Paris in 1974. At the time he was virtually a stranger, someone who for as long as she could remember had always been in a state of transit when not actually away. Her motive in going to Paris was not to rediscover him. She wanted to escape the shambles her life had degenerated into. A drug habit had crippled her studies and contributed to the break-up of her first serious sexual relationship. She was desperate and unable to turn to Patty, who was building her new family. For reasons Lauren could not explain, Patty's happiness constituted a barrier between them.

As a child she had worshipped Philip. He was the immediate expression of an exotic and fascinating world, an important person with important friends. When he was at home he lavished her with attention. But at about the time she entered adolescence this orientation was turned upside down. He spent less and less time at home, and she was increasingly exposed to Patty's unhappiness. His professional frustrations and growing dependence on drugs turned home into a place of persistent conflict, so that it was a relief when he shifted his centre of gravity irreversibly from home to his private world of night clubs, sessions and tours. At the same time, the teen culture Lauren was absorbing transformed her perception of his jazz: it was outmoded, square, an embarrassing indulgence.

Philip regretted, more deeply than he would admit, the alienation between them. He blamed himself in large part, though he recognised in her rebellion the common adolescent fight for identity. It is a natural process, he told himself, one making it easier for parents to accept that their children must find their own way in the world.

Patty divorced him as soon as Lauren left school, taking with her Lauren's family locus. Two years later Philip let the house in Stoke Poges and went to Paris. When he received her phone call there - her voice barely audible, trembling with despair - they had not seen each other for over three years.

She spent most of her summer vacation with him in the rooms he was renting near the Sorbonne. He was glad that she had turned to him, despite knowing that he was a last resort. The first week was traumatic - apart from the rearrangement of his schedule, made more difficult by an important recording date he was busy with, she was travelling a plethora of emotional slides and fighting unsuccessfully her body's dependence on drugs. Eventually he managed to get her into a rehabilitation clinic and clear his schedule sufficiently to devote most of his attention to her. For both of them it was a time of discovery and rediscovery. A new orientation to their relationship was established, a framework subsequently given flesh by the all too brief time spent exploring his Latin Quarter haunts before she had to return to the university. Their meeting, though suffused with resonances of their parent-child relationship, was essentially one between two adults.

CHAPTER 27

"You really wailed tonight."

Faith sits before the dressing-table, rubbing cream into her face with delicate movements of her middle finger. Her dark eyes, reflected in multiple images by the three mirrors, dance with a light which has burned all evening.

"Thanks, babe." Philip is lying on a double bed which, despite its plush spread, seems by its characteristic hotel coldness to invite sitting on rather than pursuits of a horizontal nature. "But *you* wowed the crowd - the woman in blue, her voice of timeless strength, her body eternally young."

She pierces him with a glare, but cannot hide her pleasure. "Stop kidding me, you old bastard."

Faith is obsessed with resisting the imprint of time. A surgeon's knife has removed its sag from her breasts, neck and face; her raven black hair is maintained by the contents of a bottle. The cracking up of her voice is more difficult to disguise, but she still convinces most audiences by her mastery of vocal colouration - she relies on exquisite timing, a bold projection of personality - her *person*, not her voice, is the point of contact - and careful emphasis on the middle registers, where the cracks are least noticeable.

In the twilight of her career, jazz has become her necessary staple. She made her name in the fifties and sixties as a singer of more enduring pop, frequently appearing and recording with bands rooted in the jazz tradition, marketed for a post-teen audience. Later she dallied in rock, but found neither the enjoyment nor the commitment to make a mark. When her voice started to fail, she returned to the only music which places a premium on qualities she still possesses in abundance - feeling and swing.

Philip has rolled onto his side, and is inserting a tape into a cassette recorder on the bedside table. He glances over his shoulder at her as the controlled richness of Louis Armstrong's trumpet rolls into the room. She smiles into her mirrors; raises her glass of brandy to his image.

"Ah, Philippe ... *santé*," she murmurs.

The tune, 'La Vie en Rose', carries special significance for them: they did it together at a gig on the night of their reunion as lovers in England, and somehow it became a signature of the relationship they have sustained since then. The trumpet ceases, and is replaced by the familiar, equally rich tones of Armstrong's voice. His words are unimportant, the simple, lilting melody bearing in itself a tender invocation of love.

Faith stands up, and, smiling at Philip, begins dancing. She wishes him to join her, but knows him well enough not to tender an invitation which will irritate him. He has always detested dancing. She closes her eyes, swaying gently with one arm about her waist, the other extended. Except for the rounded stomach, her body is slim. Only from close up can one see that age has given it a pinched appearance.

The phone rings. She glides to it, humming the song's final bars.

"Victor, darling. Doing just fine, thank you ... Phil's *always* fine - he blew *divinely* tonight ..."

The conversation is short. When it is over, she turns to Philip, a knowing smile stretching from her mouth to her arched eyebrows.

"Victor sends his love."

Philip grimaces good naturedly. "It's great to feel loved."

She switches off the light and lies down beside him. They listen to Louis Armstrong. After a long interval she places a hand on Philip's.

"Any pain tonight?"

"Nah."

She looks at him, her hand moving up his arm slowly. "*Voulez-vous coucher avec moi?*"

***

Faith had been an unmentioned presence in the discussions between Philip and Patty which led to their decision to leave Los Angeles for London. Renewed contact with her was something they both, in different ways, feared. It would move the affair of eight years before out of its position of benign assimilation in their past. But Patty was desperately unhappy in Los Angeles. Its pace, its strident rhythms, were too alien. Travel from there to South Africa for visits to her family were impossible because of the expense. And she felt excluded, past hope or desire, by Philip's musician and Beat -

144

'layabeats' she called them - friends. Their world, of intense music making, intense drinking, intense discussion, intense dope taking - everything always with intensity - threatened the peaceful rhythm of her being.

The first two or three years in London were good ones for them. He had steady work as resident tenor saxophonist at Ronnie Scott's and was persuaded by Patty into buying a semi-detached in Slough. Patty regained control of her life. She found a good job as a legal secretary, something she had been unable to do in Los Angeles, and built the home - with its garden and its pets - her work, and Lauren's school into reference points of a harmonious whole. Its rhythms were dictated by her own. Each Christmas she took Lauren with her to visit the Brennans in South Africa.

Initially Philip deliberately avoided Faith, but, reassured by Patty's calm, he soon allowed contact with her to happen naturally. They had mutual friends, saw each other at parties, and occasionally crossed paths at gigs and sessions.

In time both Philip and Patty tired of Slough's overwhelming mediocrity. With more than enough money coming in, they were able to buy the bungalow in Stoke Poges. But instead of reinforcing the domestic intimacy Patty had fashioned, it coincided with the emergence of a disenchantment which would lead to their divorce four years later. Philip was restless, increasingly hemmed in by the calm which he began to identify as control - Patty had laid down the lines and was policing them. Musically too he felt becalmed, successful but going nowhere. And his age began to bother him - he was a carthorse growing old, bound by Patty's lines to trot backwards and forwards between the city and his village pasture.

He started sleeping over in the city after gigs and taking engagements outside London whenever he could. A favourite venue of his for one-off gigs was the Man in the Moon pub in Cambridge. At one of these gigs Faith turned out to be part of the pick-up group assembled by the organiser. A surprise for Philip, as at the time she was at the height of her success as a pop singer. The moment was decisive for both of them. Musically, the gig was a rare meeting of feeling and skill, for the musicians a catharsis generated by an unsought communion of being. Faith, rollercoasting the superficial pop scene, and Philip, lacking stimulation in the jazz mainstream, felt the roots of their musicality stirred. Its juxtaposition with their marital tensions was compelling. From the outset Faith's marriage to Victor had been a loose arrangement allowing maximum freedom, sexual and otherwise. But of late Faith had been feeling increasingly insecure, sexually inhibited herself and intimidated by Victor's vigorous catholicity.

After the gig Philip invited her to have a drink with him at his hotel. They walked down the Mill Road, absorbing each other's high spirits. It was a hot summer night, an almost full moon seeming to hang immediately above them. Reminiscing about a gig impregnated with the same emotional high from their days in Pietermaritzburg, they turned onto the dark expanse of Parker's Piece, a grassed open area. They stopped at the meeting point of two paths which cut diagonally across the Piece. Examining a grotesquely decorated post which marked the point, Philip told her about his all-consuming frustration. She stretched up on her toes to kiss his cheek.

"Jesus, Phil, I'm so sorry."

Through her perfume he smelt the familiar smell of her. It was close and moist. Overwhelmed by desire, he drew her to himself.

After Cambridge they had seen each other as frequently as their professional commitments would permit. Their relationship, stable despite the fluidity of the space they allowed it, invigorated Faith's marriage. It was scarcely a factor in the already advanced disintegration of Philip's. They met like planets pursuing independent courses through the universe, infusing energies of immemorial sustenance. After Philip's divorce they briefly considered joining courses, but agreed that it would result in a destructive collision.

Cycles of closeness and distance have characterised their relationship in the intervening years - the flux and reflux of energies which, as if determined by the stars, will not allow the bond to dissipate.

CHAPTER 28

The place is almost deserted. Bored gallery attendants track the progress of the few weekday morning visitors with a diligence in inverse proportion to the visitors' numbers. Hand in hand Philip and Faith stroll through a hall of twentieth century French art. Art galleries have always been favoured meeting places of theirs - the Tate or the National Portrait Gallery in London, the Jeu de Paume in Paris - and shelters from bad weather. Today they are in the Johannesburg Art Gallery at Lauren's suggestion. At last night's gig, which she and Ed attended, she invited them to share lunch with her in the Gallery restaurant. Her office is just around the corner, in a shabby Hillbrow block of mainly neglected residential buildings. For her, last night was a great success. She had arrived at the club in a state of nervous tension. But Faith's relaxed friendliness disarmed her; made their first meeting since her adolescence as pleasurable as nervousness would allow. And Ed, for whom first impressions are always clear-cut, thought her winsome.

Philip stops as they exit the hall; gazes intently at a sculpted bust in an alcove across the passageway. It is a Rodin in whitest marble. As he leads Faith to it, an attendant steps out of the hall after them.

"Christ, these characters give me the creeps," Philip mutters. "Give me an Italian gallery any time."

As he remembers them, attendants in Italy are sparse, more interested in their navels or conversations with colleagues than in the crowds of visitors.

"He'll probably wet his pants if I touch this thing."

Faith smiles, shaking her head, then turns abruptly to the attendant.

"Excuse me. Please would you direct me to the toilet."

Impassively he moves down the passage, his large body squeezed into a uniform designed for someone a lot smaller than him. Winking at Philip, Faith follows him.

Philip immediately stretches out a hand to the serene image of Miss Fairfax. He strokes the smooth, cool stone. It seems to connect with the pain in his chest, a malevolent alien expanding dully with each breath. He toys with the idea of willing it into the stone, but Miss Fairfax is too beautiful.

His thoughts are drawn back to the charged emotion of last night's gig, where the meeting between Faith and Lauren was overshadowed by the reunion with Ray Gamede. Philip had known he would be there. While still in London he had enquired after him, and having established that he was around, requested the club owner to do his best to include Ray in the programme. The reunion was an emotional one. Philip had almost walked into him as he entered the club's foyer. Ray was facing the other way, his trumpet case held loosely behind his back. His tall, slightly stooped figure seemed to lean over the person he was talking to. Philip noticed a faint peppering of grey in his hair.

"How's the old man doing?" he said softly.

Still talking, Ray half turned. His face ignited with a flashing of eyes and teeth. Laughing delightedly, he enveloped Philip in a bear hug, the trumpet case dangling against Philip's hip.

"So, you have come back."

He released Philip and took his hand. They looked at each other. Words failed them both, the joy in their faces saying whatever had to be said.

Playing again with Ray was a moving experience. The sharp phrasing Philip remembered was absent, and his distinctively bop sound had been replaced by a township lyricism. But Philip had deliberately brought no expectations to the gig. Being together, swinging together, was all that mattered. And they swung. Despite the pain in his chest, Philip blew a celebratory gale which the rest of the band rode into the morning.

He is still standing in front of Miss Fairfax when Faith returns. She takes his hand.

"Shall we move on? Lauren will be here soon."

They have arranged to meet in a courtyard leading off the bottom level of halls. As they pass the tightly-fitted, vigilant attendant again, Philip says to him, "Fred Splinge will be here in an hour, dad."

"Huh?"

"In an hour," Philip emphasizes, as Faith hurries him away.

She giggles. "You crazy bastard."

They see Lauren through the sheets of glass which separate the courtyard from the halls. She is sitting on a bench, gazing at an outsize sculpture of a nude girl. Behind her, enclosing the courtyard, is an artificial waterfall. She sits as still as a statue before the dancing water.

***

"God, it was a scream. We all got a little drunk - some of us more than a little," Faith looks pointedly at Philip. "Victor was making passes at this young girl, I forget her name - we called her the tinsel tart - she wore make-up and dressed just like me, you see - and her partner was doing the same to me. They got very competitive about it, until Victor won the day by offering the tinsel tart a carnation he stole from an adjacent table. My admirer took it rather badly. Believe it or not, he snatched the carnation away and *ate* the fucking thing."

She is telling Lauren about the surprise dinner party she organised for Philip's fiftieth birthday.

"Of course, the only respectable people there were your mother and her husband."

Lauren laughs. "Ja, I can imagine."

Her elbows on the table, she sits leaned over her plate of vegetarian pie, her eyes following Faith's every movement.

"But it was your mother who broke us all up. Except Philip, who by that stage was close to passing out." She pauses to watch a couple pass their table. "She was sitting next to the carnation eater. After his little act, she procured another one, and, very formally, handed it to him with the comment, 'I believe they're not very filling.'"

They all laugh. Lauren smiles at Philip. She detains a stray lock of hair and flips it back behind her ear.

"You never did like dinner parties," she says.

He shakes his head. "One of my allergies." He looks down at his half empty plate, smiling apologetically. "This is good stuff, but I'm not very hungry."

"Another of his allergies," Faith says as she spears the last of her sole, "is gallery attendants."

She relates their encounter with him of the tight-fitting uniform. The afternoon sun has crept across to their table. It glosses the movements of Faith's head and silk blouse, which falls elegantly from her elbows. Visible through the window behind her is the gallery's inner courtyard with its stretch of lawn tastefully decorated by trees and sculptures. Most of it is cast in a deep shadow warm with the greenness of the grass.

Philip is detached. His thoughts wander, are drawn back to the pain in his chest, wander again. The sun highlights the messy halo emanating from the cigarette he holds close to his face. He considers how different the two women are. And how different the ties which link each to him. The tentative contact happening between them pleases him. In his mind it forges a triangle reflecting their physical arrangement around the small table.

They are talking about their tastes in music. There are many superficially strange convergences - the Beatles, Cream, Jethro Tull, Pink Floyd, Sting. They are attempting to identify the common thread when their coffees arrive.

"Thank God," Philip says. "I feel parched listening to you two."

"Aren't you just so *fucking* superior," Faith teases.

Lauren is stirring her coffee. Without looking up, she says, "Why don't you two get married?"

Faith's laugh seems to tinkle in the sun. "But darling, we *are* married."

Lauren looks at Philip.

"We are joined in the marriage of minds, the thing Shakespeare was into. And of bodies, naturally." Again the tinkling laugh. "Legal marriage *never* works, unless you stretch it into the kind of thing Victor and I have. And then, strictly speaking, it's no longer marriage."

"It's worked for Ed and me."

Philip gazes at Lauren, inscrutable behind his dark glasses. "The exception that proves the rule, honeybee."

Faith fiddles with her teaspoon. "Excuse my ranting, darling. Of course there are exceptions. I suppose Philip and I just don't rate our chances at becoming exceptions."

CHAPTER 29

Switch on the TV, open a newspaper, listen to a conversation in a pub, tune in to the word games in your own head, the term keeps popping up - 'the New South Africa'. For the powerful it is a tool to suggest that the transformation of society has already happened; for those still fighting *apartheid* it is a two-edged promise of success; to the reactionaries it is blasphemy; and for most ordinary people it is that fly buzzing against the window pane which you just can't catch. During the gig in Pietermaritzburg at the Ansonia I wondered what was new about an audience in which I couldn't see one black face. Here in the Hillbrow I've been walking all afternoon I see something which has grown old, you know, being new. It is a place of cosmopolitan texture, teeming with languages and colours, mostly black. Typically of modern inner cities - Christ, it reminds me of downtown LA - vitality rubs shoulders with squalor. This is not the South Africa I remember. Older than the 'New South Africa', it is the face of something new.

As I round a corner and see my hotel up ahead, I feel old. People who say that age is an attitude of mind are talking shit. When your body starts packing up, having a youthful approach to life means fuck all - in anybody's terms you are *old*. Yesterday I saw a doctor about the pain in my chest, and this morning he gave me the results of all the tests he did. A hiatus hernia, effectively incurable.

"Mr Maddox, let me be brutally honest with you," this slick young cat said to me. "With medication you can live with it, to a ripe old age if your poor lungs don't give in." He stared disapprovingly at the packet of Texans in my pocket. "But playing a trumpet... sorry, a saxophone, for a living is not part of that scenario. You are going to have to retire, I'm afraid."

And take up stamp collecting, I suppose. I asked him what would happen if I just kept blowing. He whipped his hand across his throat.

"At the end of the day, you understand. You could probably keep going for a while, but the pain would become unbearable eventually."

I reach the hotel entrance, but still cannot face talking to anyone, even Faith. The pedestrian light at the corner is green, and I run to make it. I walk a block on the other side before crossing into Joubert

Park. The sun has slipped behind the taller buildings as I catch my breath ambling down a wide path towards the Art Gallery. Bird song and car hooters play the upper registers. The rest of the scale is filled by the rise and fall of traffic noise.

The first time I can remember feeling old was during the sixties, when Patty and I were still together. Christ, if only I'd known. At times the sense of slowing down, you know, of being locked into a phase of unending mediocrity, was suffocating. I fought it by chasing young chicks; pushing my blowing wherever it would take me; abandoning everything, including Patty, which offered me safe options. Now I know that slowing down is something you can handle. The ultimate enemy, the harbinger of death, is physical sickness. Haemorrhoids I've had plenty of. Two bouts of pneumonia. Now it's a hernia; next it will be trembling hands, incontinence, senility. There are some strange things in the world, but something you will never find is a cool incontinent. Christ. When sickness has taken away your dignity, death is a release. It is your friend.

I stop at the strip of paving running in front of the Gallery. The pale stone of the low building is almost pink in the subtle illumination of dusk. I hear the sound of running water. Ahead of me is an artificial waterfall, its water falling into the courtyard below. It is dominated by a bronze nude, a girl stretching her arms above her head luxuriously. I haul out a Texan, and looking down at the nude who is glaringly *young*, smoke it with fierce, deep inhalations. Surely there is no celebration more meaningful than that which guided the hands of this sculptor. In a few minutes the Texan is finished, and peevishly I flick it into the courtyard.

I remember a night long ago when I walked alone in the darkness of a strange farmyard. A sense of alienation divested me of any awareness of being cool; rendered the very notion of coolness absurd. The same thing is happening to me now. To be cool, rather to *feel* cool, you must engage your immediate world. Sickness fashions alienation in perhaps the most fundamental form of engagement - between you and your body. A *dead* man has a better chance of being cool than a sick man. Jesus, I'm not making sense. I'm afraid.

Faith will be waiting for me. I turn from the courtyard and walk quickly back the way I came. Lights illuminate the path now, and all around the darkened park is a barrier of illuminated windows and street lights. I am almost at the exit when I hear raised voices. Under a tree some way from the path is a knot of tramps. They talk in slurred shouts as they divide up something one of them is taking from a plastic carrier bag. I hurry on, disturbed by the thought that essentially they are no different from me. Merely more committed to the spurning of ties which give a semblance of significance to our lives, to the embrace of the vagrancy which ultimately none of us can avoid.

"Where *have* you been?" Faith asks as I enter our room. "I was beginning to get worried."

She sits in her underwear at the dressing-table, making up her face for tonight's gig. I stand behind her, my hands on her shoulders.

"Just walking."

She leans forward to do something to her eyes. "Shall I ask room-service to send up sandwiches?"

Neither of us digs a big meal before a gig.

Placing my hands under her elbows, I lift her up. She turns, and I take her in my arms. Her body is pathetically thin, but I know it well and it feels good.

She whispers, "Is the man passionate?"

I hold her more tightly.

CHAPTER 30

Ray manoeuvres his car, a frequently and inexpertly panel-beaten Toyota, out of the yard. Rain, sun and vehicles have worked the dirt into a hard labyrinth of tracks. As it bumps its pot-holed way onto the road, a group of children standing outside the gate shout enthusiastic greetings. Philip, bouncing in the passenger seat, does not recognise them from the workshop which has just ended.

"Kids waiting for their drama classes," Ray says, swinging the car across to allow a minibus taxi with flashing lights to pass.

On the back of the taxi Philip notices the name Zola Budd painted in decorative script. Alongside it is an 'I love Hopeville' sticker with a red heart depicting love. Philip points at the rapidly disappearing vehicle.

"Another wild taxi driver," he says. "I wonder if Hopeville loves him."

Ray chuckles to himself.

"How long've you been involved with these workshops?" Philip asks.

"We go back a long way. I was there when the Community Centre started - I don't know, maybe ten years. It was very small then. Not much money, and unfortunately the people were ignorant. They had to be educated to understand what we were trying to achieve."

Philip nods, the while opening a new box of cigarettes. He offers it to Ray.

"Ai! No thanks. I have won that battle."

"Jesus Christ, not another health fanatic!" He puts the box back in his pocket. "Judging by the turn-out we got today, you must have done a good job of educating people."

"Well, you can say so, although we have had ups and downs. Actually, during the state of emergency we had to close down for a long time. When we started moving again we had to sweat to find funds. But in the last two years we have been using this..." He points to his temple. "We work with the Civic, the women's organisation, the youth, and other community organisations. When they support a project ..."

"What's the Civic?"

Ray grins at him. "Ai, but you are a fokken uitlander now. They are our community leaders. The government tried to force one of their puppet local councils on us, but the people rejected it." He shakes his head. "Those were bad days."

"A lot of violence?"

"Bad, bad. We have all suffered."

Philip looks at him, but he does not elaborate. They stop at a shambolic intersection - there are no stop signs, roads come into it at crazy angles, and the vehicles, mainly taxis, jockey for position in a cacophony of hooting. While they wait their turn to brave the crossing, two pedestrians dodge the traffic to reach the Toyota. Ray introduces them to Philip, then speaks to them briefly in a language he does not recognise.

The workshop was the first of three arranged for Philip, another two in Soweto completing the programme. It is a new experience for him. As he sits in the car, it is still too soon to have assimilated it. He has never enjoyed formal teaching, although in recent years it has become an increasingly important supplementary source of income for him. But it is always in an intimate, one to one framework. The dozen or so students in his class at the Centre were intimidating.

The other musician on the trip, a pianist, also participated in the workshop. It started with brief lessons conducted by the Centre's usual teachers, the two visitors observing in order to get a feel for things. They then each conducted classes in their fields of competence - the pianist did piano and the rhythm section, while Philip covered reed instruments. After a short break, during which the visitors were surrounded by students plying them with questions, refreshments and requests for autographs, the workshop ended with a demonstration session. Here the visitors were joined by teachers and one or two star pupils, and for the first time Philip began to relax. He was given the honour of closing proceedings - to his relief, no speech was expected - with a number of his choice. 'Climb Every Mountain' was his selection, which he played in front of a three-piece rhythm section. His blowing was far removed from the warm, soothing tones of the classic rendition by Coleman Hawkins. Instead he used it to blow his anger at the pain which threatened to take his horn from him forever.

***

For years after he left Pietermaritzburg in 1955 Ray maintained strong ties with his family home. No important decision could be taken in the Edendale house without the family first consulting him, so his trips home, always by overnight train, were frequent. But his involvement rested on far more than merely his sense of duty - he missed his mother, the other family members, his friends in the Swingsters, the whole community. He was shaped by a culture in which individual affirmation is found primarily through the practice of community. Though his decision to leave was arrived at communally - never did he regard it as a private matter - the consequence undermined the basis of his affirmation. Until he was able to root himself in a new community, he laboured with a sense of identity in pieces. The process was one which Philip would never understand.

Ray's move to Johannesburg was almost still-born. A room had been organised for him in Sophiatown, from where he was to find a bigger place before his wife and children joined him. Within months it became obvious that Sophiatown was doomed, its existence deemed undesirable by the lords of *apartheid*. Facing destruction together with it was the vibrant culture which the community had given birth to. Homesick and struggling to put down new roots, Ray almost gave up the venture. But his band, the Big City Stompers, drew him into their joint resolve to survive. They moved base to Hopeville, from where they took their Sophiatown sound to all corners of the Rand. However, they steadily lost dates in the city, and by the late fifties state action to destroy everything associated with Sophiatown culture saw an end to their radio broadcasts and recording work. But they survived. Ray settled his family in Hopeville, and by doing well at work ensured that he was not dependent on the band for a livelihood. After his mother died he returned less frequently to Edendale, over the years becoming part of Hopeville through the practice of neighbourhood and the practice of community.

The band finally dissolved in the late seventies, after which Ray played casually whenever and wherever he felt like blowing. A well-known figure in the township, he was invited to participate as an organiser and teacher when the Community Centre was being established. He agreed, and became an integral part of the Centre's voluntary management. In the last two years, with better funding and community support, he has been paid for his services.

***

Philip pats the shoulder of the small boy who has given him the distinctive three-part township handshake.

"Teaser," Ray introduces his grandson. "A proud comrade and tireless teaser of his sisters."

Philip stands in the lounge of Ray's small but comfortable house. Before him, having proffered their greetings, are Ray's wife and three of his grandchildren.

"Let us not stand here forever." Ray gestures towards a chair. "What about a beer?"

They are seated when his wife returns with a tray bearing two tankards of beer and a plate of biscuits. She smiles at Philip as he inspects its contents.

"I remember you, Mr Maddox. The *umlungu*." She giggles.

He smiles. "Phil, please."

And then she is gone, leaving the two men to talk. Which they do, mainly about jazz, a little about the 'New South Africa'. Their conversation is punctuated by the rise and fall of the children's subdued voices as they play on the floor. Ray's wife comes in repeatedly to check that the children are not becoming a nuisance and to replenish their tankards.

Philip's reticence about his private life is picked up immediately by Ray, and he studiously avoids referring to the subject. The conversation meanders on safe terrain, neither discovering more than a vague outline of the other's experience since their days together in Pietermaritzburg. Philip learns nothing of the Gamede's trauma during the township uprising in the eighties. The death of their youngest son in a confrontation between demonstrators and the police. The constant fear which becomes normal. Ray's three months in detention.

They are interrupted by visitors. After speaking to them briefly at the front door, Ray asks Philip to excuse him.

"There is a small problem. A neighbourhood matter."

Left by himself, Philip explores the room. He stops before the hi-fi set, which is stacked on a cabinet containing Ray's collection of records. He squats down and works his way through it, taking each record out carefully one at a time. He stops when he discovers one of his own recordings. It dates back to his years in Los Angeles. He takes it to his chair, where he is reading the sleeve notes when Ray returns.

"Ai, that is my favourite!" he exclaims, beaming. "Let me put it on."

As he fusses in front of the hi-fi, Philip pulls out a cigarette.

"Would you mind?" he asks, holding it up.

"By all means. You mustn't ask. Every day I have neighbours in here, and not one is health conscious." He smiles. "We are, after all, a third world country."

For a while they concentrate on listening to the record. It is a beautiful recording of Philip playing with the Hampton Hawes Trio, one of the most swinging outfits in the fifties West Coast scene. Philip has not listened to it in years, and is moved by what he hears.

"Ray, would you stop blowing if a doctor told you you must?"

He describes the scenario explained to him a week ago.

Ray pushes a forefinger into his widow's peak. "It is a hard thing, Phil. Yes, I would." He continues after a long pause. "It does not have to be the end of your music. You have a wonderful gift to pass on to the youth."

CHAPTER 31

From the hotel window I watch morning finding itself again in the street below. Two more and we'll be back in London. The thought makes me weary - that fundamental rhythm of life, endings overtaken by beginnings, is leaving me behind. I can just make out the words on the billboard at the street corner - HOSTELS ERUPT 35 DEAD. The plainness of those ciphers, the peacefulness of the cityscape, seem to magnify the horror. I look away, gripped by a sense of unreality. The vendor, a black kid, whistles his wares at the few cars which stop when the lights turn red.

"You alright, Phil?"

Faith is watching me from the bed.

"Yeah." I attempt a smile.

"Come back to me. You're getting up at uncivilised hours these days."

But the street draws me away. I turn to it and the insignificant obscenity which seems to challenge its very existence. My brain is a whirl of questions. Ever since we arrived in South Africa I've been holding down the lid on them. Is this part of being here at a time when the old, apparently impregnable laager is collapsing? Or is it a personal scene, the citadel of my consciousness beginning to crack open under the pressure of a new reality? The fucking terror of being abandoned by my body.

I go to Faith, press her head against mine.

"I need to see Ray again. You mind if I try to set something up for today?"

"Baby," she whispers, holding me tightly.

***

Ray agrees to pick me up at the hotel after lunch. It is a Saturday, and there is an afternoon gig at a downtown jazz club. We arrive early enough to watch the musicians setting up their instruments at the back of this cramped joint with plenty of character. I choose a table as far from the bandstand as possible. He tells me about the cats who will be playing, then asks me how my other workshops went. After a couple of brandies I begin to relax.

"The other day, at your place," I plunge in, not knowing whether I'll find the right words. "I was really uptight, you know what I mean? Kind of dislocated, not with you at all. I'm sorry."

Ray smiles wryly, shaking his head. "No apologies, Phil. That is where I was too."

The band is beginning to settle into a swinging groove, and for a moment we both dig it. Then we talk, about the things I avoided with him the other day and other stuff caught in the web of my diffidence. We are locked in an intense embrace by my urgency. I am relentless in pursuit of the release of pressure in my brain, aware all the time of the afternoon draining away from us. Ray's story provides no answers. If anything, it raises a host of new questions. But hearing him tell it, and telling him my own, soothes the fever. It is good to get up close to him again.

The last set has begun before I lay off. Ray has taken a trip to the can, and for the first time I've allowed myself to absorb the atmosphere of the joint. The air is dense with sound and smoke. The floor is wall to wall humanity, the faces mostly black and dizzy with animation. I gesture toward it all.

"This is what we should have got together in Pietermaritzburg."

Ray grins, but there is weariness in his eyes. "You are right, brother. The time, you can say, was not with us though."

I shake my head as I haul out another smoke. My mouth tastes like a gravel-pit. I ask Ray about the Interim Cultural Desk. He concedes that it has problems, but argues that it performs a necessary and important function.

"Sure, dad, that I can understand. It is the way they operated with us that got on my tits."

"Phil, you have been away a long time. There are processes happening here which you must see arising from a specific situation. How can I say?" He jabs a finger nervously at his forehead. "When people have not had a voice for so long, when they find it you must expect them to miss the key sometimes and disagree on the harmony. Phil, finding the voice is the important thing. Don't despise it."

I consider his words. Here is a guy, despite everything, at peace with his world.

"At the Community Centre it is the same," he continues. "Some of the people I work with don't understand cultural work. And there are others who do but have their own agendas. It can be difficult. But we are moving. Against everything that is trying to stop us, we are moving."

He leans towards me, his hands clasped around his empty glass. Behind him a big white chick in kind of hippy dress is leaning precariously against a diminutive black cat. Her long hair spills down his back.

"Ray, I don't know. I'm not connecting."

He chuckles. "Brother, you never did."

It is dusk when he drops me back at the hotel. Hillbrow is lighting up, and the energy on its pavements is being drawn in for the evening razzle. I feel tired as I watch the tail-lights of the Toyota disappear into the stream of traffic. A memory from long ago surfaces, of Ray and me parting outside his home in Edendale. Beginnings beckoned us both then, holding for us divergent journeys. All this time for the wheel to turn.

A taxi pulls in at the curb, its hooting wrenching me back into the present. I walk to the hotel entrance, aware suddenly of being hungry and needing the touch of Faith's body against mine.

CHAPTER 32

Perhaps because I'm pretty self-centred I've always found it easy to make decisions. Which pair of trousers to buy, whether to quit a band or not, the answer seems to present itself without my having to extract it. Faith is the same. And, come to think of it, Patty too. I have little patience for the weighing of possible consequences, the careful consideration of other peoples' interests, and, after the decision is finally made, doubts about whether it was the right one. But that's where I'm at now, as much as I tell myself that the problem doesn't require the making of a decision - I must do what I have to do, and fuck consequences. Who knows, maybe that slick doctor has got it wrong. I'll get a second opinion as soon as I'm back home.

I look at the two books I've placed on the table - the Terence Conran, which I've hardly looked at since arriving, and a novel by Milan Kundera. The novel I bought a few days ago in Hillbrow for reading in the shithouse, the Conran giant being rather awkward for that purpose. I am digging this cynical, amusing cat the most - besides, you know, he's good for my bowels. As I pick him up I notice Ed smiling at me from the other side of the table.

The three of us are relaxing on the patio after a lunch I can only describe as shitty. Lauren prepared the light meal as a kind of illustration of how interesting health foods can be - a salad containing strange beans and other inedible bits of vegetable, a homemade loaf of bread full of seeds or something, and bowls of yoghurt sprinkled with nuts and honey. I think I'm going to need Kundera when it all comes out the other end.

The patio leads onto a secluded area almost entirely filled by a swimming pool of unusual shape, being formed by three interlinking rectangles of different sizes. The sun sparkles on the water, which is disturbed by a monster dully chugging across the pool's bottom. According to Ed it is a kind of vacuum cleaner. While neighbouring houses are entirely concealed by a combination of elevation and dense hedges, from the patio there is an expansive view across the wooded northern suburbs of Johannesburg.

Ed has looked up from the pile of papers resting on his lap. The reading glasses placed low on his nose look kind of incongruous against the healthy tan of his face.

"A story I think you would enjoy, Phil." He prods the papers. "This guy I'm defending. He's a relatively minor figure on the national stage, a township activist, with very hardline Marxist views. Soon after I was given the case, he told me that as far as he was concerned the only significant thing to have come out of the first meeting between the government and the ANC was that Joe Slovo smokes Benson and Hedges Special Mild and wears grey slip-on shoes. For him it confirmed that Slovo was courting upper middle-class whites and the security establishment - you wouldn't know this, but grey shoes are standard wear in the security police."

I smile disbelievingly. "You being serious?"

Ed laughs. "Absolutely." He points at the book in my hands. "Kundera would find a lot of material in South Africa."

He glances at his watch. "Christ, I'm going to be late."

The two spaniels which have been sleeping under the table scramble out when he gets up. They watch him expectantly as he puts on his jacket and disposes of his glasses. He bends to kiss Lauren.

"See you at the club, probably after nine," he says, departing in a flurry of paws and barks.

Lauren smiles at me in the quiet they leave behind. She reclines on a deck-chair, in vest and shorts, her brown legs stretched out in the sun.

I nod in the direction of Ed's departure. "Is this routine for a Sunday afternoon?"

"Ja, it's part of the job to work strange hours. He also gets called out a lot, less so since the end of the emergency."

I fiddle with the silver-plated lighter Lauren and Ed have given me. Lauren slipped it into my hands this morning with the words, "It's a Guy Fawkes present" - an old family joke, derived from Max's habit of wishing people happy Guy Fawkes at any special occasion.

"It doesn't bother you, Lol?"

"One gets used to it. Besides, I'm out often myself - evening meetings, conferences, field trips, that kind of thing."

I slap the lighter down on Kundera, shaking my head. "Fucking missionaries."

"Oh c'mon, Phil, hardly. Anyway, you're a fine one to talk." She reaches down to pat one of the returned spaniels. "If it's commitment you're talking about, you take some beating."

I ponder that one for a moment. Of course I'm committed to my horn, but I play for myself, not in pursuit of an idea or for the benefit of society.

"My music is about self-fulfilment, you know. Obviously it involves all kinds of sharing - with fellow musicians, with audiences - but it happens out of a sense of responsibility to myself. You dig what I'm saying? The responsibility is not to other people."

It is her turn to ponder, which she does by chewing a fingernail. Her other hand rests on the spaniel, which has flopped down beneath her just out of the sun.

"Phil, I hear what you're saying. But I would argue that we all have a responsibility to society, a practical one more than a moral one. For myself, and I think I can speak for Ed as well, fulfilling that responsibility is a way of fulfilling responsibility to ourselves. There has to be a balance, though ultimately I suppose self-fulfilment must come first. Am I making sense?"

"Sure. I think I'm with you."

"When we were younger the balance was probably skew. The struggle was more important than anything else." She pauses, her gaze lifted up over the pool. "Then again, I wonder if it wasn't just our need for self-fulfilment expressing itself in a different way."

I stand up; stretch out my arms. She watches me, a gentle smile on her lips.

"So what you're suggesting - am I right? - is that the incredible self-sacrifice of a Mother Theresa is really an expression of her own need for self-fulfilment," I ask.

"Ja." She nods. "I suppose so."

This is heavy stuff, not the kind of thing I normally enjoy talking about. But I'm in a weird mood today. After Lauren has made us tea, and a vain attempt to get into Kundera, I find myself pursuing the heavy line.

"You and Ed still not planning on having kids?"

She puts her paperback down. "You're not wanting grandchildren are you?"

"Nah - you know me. Just interested."

"No, we're not."

She's obviously not wildly enthusiastic about the topic, but I'm feeling bloody-minded.

"Well, as long as you agree on it."

She nods. "Our reasons are slightly different. For Ed it's a philosophical question - the decision to give life to someone when for most people life means unhappiness, is one he doesn't feel able to take. My reasons are more complex, but essentially I think that what we have together is too special to risk spoiling."

I've been doing a lot of pondering today. I dig my watch as I let the thoughts tumble. Faith will be arriving soon.

"Faith was against having kids until she was about your age. Then she tried to fall pregnant but couldn't. Eventually she went to a gynaecologist, who told her there was some problem which made it impossible."

Am I warning her? Merely inviting comment on what was for me a troubling scene? I don't know, but whatever, my words are way out of court.

Lauren stands up. "For us it's no longer an issue - Ed's had a vasectomy." She walks over to the pool. "Phil, would you mind if I have a swim?"

I shake my head.

She strips off. I notice that she is brown all over. She dives in and swims the longest length with elegant but firm strokes. At the other end she stops, just her head above the surface.

"Come and join me," she calls. "The water's great."

"No thanks, honeybee. It would kill me."

"You old ninny."

She takes off again. I imagine jumping into the cool embrace of the water; of sliding slowly to the bottom, turning and turning, the sunlit world far above me; watching the air escape from me until I am empty of it; and a peaceful oblivion - in which no decisions have to be made, where there is no sickness or frailty - possessing me.